WHAT H[

The cover picture is an enlargement of Joan Hassall's wood-engraving, *Reflections*. The end-pieces and decorations are wood-engravings by Monica Poole (*A dandelion* and *A wild-rose*), Edwina Ellis (*A leafy grove*), Ian Stephens (from *A Deserted Garden*) and Joan Hassall (*Singing Birds*). The marshland bird and the two end-papers are by Christopher Fiddes.

Except for the Dedication which, properly, is set in Baskerville, the type fount used is Garamond.

WHAT HETTY DID

or

LIFE AND LETTERS

JAMES CARR

J. L. CARR   THE QUINCE TREE PRESS   KETTERING

WHAT HETTY DID

First published in England in 1988

Copyright © by J. L. Carr

ISBN 0 900847 91 3

This is one of an edition of 3,000 copies and, although two hundred and thirty-five publications originated at this establishment under another name, is the first (and perhaps the last) book published by the Quince Tree Press.

J. L. CARR   PUBLISHER   27 MILL DALE ROAD
KETTERING

This is a Printing Office,
Cross-roads of Civilisation,
Refuge of all the Arts against the Ravages of Time.
From this place Words may fly abroad
Not to perish as Waves of Sound but fix'd in Time,
Not corrupted by the hurrying Hand but verified in Proof.
Friend, you are on Safe Ground:
This is a Printing Office.

Photoset and printed in Great Britain by
Stanley L. Hunt (Printers) Ltd. Rushden, Northamptonshire

'Dauntless the slug-horn to my lips I set
And blew – "Childe Roland to the Dark Tower came."

Robert Browning and William Shakespeare.

'Have you no mind to do what nobody can do for you?'

Miguel de Cervantes – Don Quixote.

'Put her in a room with any six people old enough to be her
parents and her parents may be there for anything she
knows. They may be in any house she sees, they may be in
any churchyard she passes, she may run against 'em in any
street and never know it. She knows nothing about 'em.
Never did. Never will.'

Charles Dickens – Little Dorrit.

James Lloyd Carr attended the village school at Carlton
Miniott in the North Riding and Castleford Secondary
School. He lives in Northamptonshire.

For A, H, P, S, M and N and for many a landlady gone
but unforgotten.
And also for Edmund Kirby who,
in his ninety-eighth year,
showed unwearied interest
in the production of this book
which
is dedicated to the Memory of John Baskerville
of Birmingham,
who designed this type fount,
invented wove paper
and lost money cheerfully on particular books which he published.

These people appear elsewhere

George Harpole, Emma Foxberrow, Miss Tollemache, Mr
Pintle, Croser, Billitt in *The Harpole Report* and two of them
go off to *Sinji*. Their middle history will be found in *Harpole
& Foxberrow, Publishers*, still unwritten.

Edward Peplow, Brightwell, Bellenger, Ruskin, Mullett and
Dexter in *A Day in Summer*.

Mr Fangfoss, Poor Beattie and Gidner come from *Steeple
Sinderby* and Gidner's uncle from *The Battle of Pollocks
Crossing*. There is mention of Miss Witherpen in *A Month in
the Country*.

A Passage of Arms

Of course, although I didn't know that it was the beginning of the end, I recall the circumstances exactly. It was Saturday and the four of us were sitting at our table pushed beneath the front-room window and making do with minced scrag-end. I even remember that Mum was boasting that nobody, nobody at all, could ('Could they Dad?') tell her plastic tablecloth from real linen.

"Just look at that sort of blush pink criss-cross. Nobody would ('Would they Dad?') tell it's not wove into it."

These appeals for confirmation from Authority were rhetorical; she would have been swooningly grateful for even a grunt or, more likely, a yelp – for Dad was a fox-terrier breed of man, all jump, bristle and bite. But this time his response was startling: he sprang to his feet and yelled fiercely, "There! Look! Just look! Layabouts! The lot of them! All on the Social Security! Blasted long-haired parasites!"

In our house, when the One jumped, all jumped. But it was only another sad little band of CND Ban-the-Bomb protesters trudging past, doggedly heading towards the American missile base. A sodden procession had been trailing through Jordans Bank for the last couple of hours but his ill-temper was not exhausted. (How could it, being inexhaustible?) Yet, once more, the window-pane would have absorbed his venom had not a rough-haired mongrel dashed into the garden in pursuit of my stray and secret cat (who, as I well knew, could look after himself).

He kicked back a chair and raged into the downpour. "Out! Get out, blast you" he screamed, slashing with his walking-stick so that the silly creature swerved and scuttled for refuge into the tabernacle itself, his greenhouse. And, of course, there it was cornered and in for a thrashing, although the first swipe only brought low a couple of overfed tomato plants.

But something equally theatrical was afoot: a tall gaunt woman in a venerable burberry burst through our snicket-gate and charged to the rescue.

"Do not dare, you appalling bully," she cried in imperious tones. "Do not dare. Do you hear me? Lay but one finger upon my dawg and I shall prosecute you – if need be, through every court in this land. Here Mustafa, good little dawg, come here."

Each glared furiously at the other. Then she marched past him, brought down another tomato plant whilst rummaging for her animal and turned again. And saw me. It was Miss Braceburn.

I prayed (with no confidence at all), "O Lord, let Monday never come." For her eyes had registered, 'Ah, Hetty Birtwisle' and I could have sunk beneath the doorstep. Yet my next thought was that, if Monday must come, then at least I could tell Mariana that Miss Braceburn had a little dawg called Mustafa.

She scornfully tossed her college scarf over a shoulder and, head high, strode back to join the marchers. These, engrossed in their own damp misery, still probed forward to make contact with the enemy's outer pickets.

"No, no, no, I don't want any of your blasted sago pudding," Dad yelled at Mum. "And don't stand there gawping. Where's your wits, woman? Get after her and take her name and address so as I can have her summonsed for criminal damage." Then, banging the door, he went round the house to mourn defeat amongst our few dejected hens. He knew that he had been bested. Worse, he knew that I knew.

I should like to have remarked how upset Dad became

4

over next to nothing but well (only too well) knew Sonny (my twelve-year-old brother) would misreport me. So I helped myself to the rejected pudding until Mum, soaked and downtrodden, sidled in. But she perked up, recognizing that, for the moment, she could delay grovelling for her mission's failure.

"They all look the same in this rain, Ethel," she complained. "You can't tell men from women. And how was I to know her again when all I could think of at the time was his tomato plants. I did ask, but nobody knew nobody else because they're here from all over the shop. And when I did ask, some spoke that queer you could hardly make out what they were on about."

A girlish excitement momentarily lit her pale eyes. "There was a big black woman. You should have seen her gold earrings. What whoppers! And you should have seen her teeth when she laughed! She was in a sort of yellow turban and it was running down her face. The dye was. But didn't she laugh!"

"I'm just going along to Polly's to return a Latin text we have to share for homework," I said. "If Dad asks, say I shan't be away long."

"Don't you get wet, our Ethel," she called mechanically. Then I hurried into the blue gaberdine raincoat already eighteen months too short for me, jammed on a fisherman's sou'wester the Major had made me accept – and joined the marchers.

5

Peace at any Price

Some carried banners,

ABERTILLERY SPEAKS PEACE

BERMONDSEY AGAINST THE A-BOMB

OLDHAM & ROCHDALE ANIMAL RIGHTS ACTIVISTS

But none, far-flung as they were, could have come up against country like ours – onion fields, spud and beet fields, mile and mile after mile of hedgeless flatness, dykes and ditches, with crossroad finger-posts pointing towards places like Poulter's Guelph and Forty Foot Drain to those travellers who hadn't drowned already.

I pushed my way through a retreating bunch of chips-with-everything beer-bellies whose dejected banner proclaimed them Sons of the Jarrow Marchers until I hove up by a hairy giant.

"Bloody bogland!" he groused. "No wonder the peasants have faces like frogs. Which lot are you with? Not that piss-and-wind gang from Scargill-Land I hope."

"Putney Philosophical and Debating Society" I lied.

"Middle-class bleedinghearts, forever passing resolutions and fuckall else! You should affiliate with us activists. Have a bash first: talk later. What's your scene?"

"Republicans," I told him. "We are the last republicans. The Civil War Putney Army Debates, you know."

"I don't know" the revolting man snarled. "Putney!"

"Then you should know," I said fiercely, working up loyalty to a name known only from Boat Race Day (and, at the same time, resolving to look into the possibilities of republicanism – being sick of Princess Diana forever on TV in new outfits).

"Come back to Darlington in my banger before Special Branch get a line on you. I go for redheads with long legs. I've got a subsidized council pad up there. We could pool the Dole. And I'm good in bed."

I dropped back and joined a parson, his loyal wife and their three young children. I can't imagine what the kids must have been thinking. But none was howling, recognizing I suppose that there was no chance of being bought-off with an ice-lolly. On the other hand, they may have decided that it was less awful than being dragged around some church bazaar.

The Vicar was an intellectual. "The lone and level beet fields stretched far away" he misquoted. "Yet folk live here!"

Live here! Good heavens, why ever not! I thought, for Fenland was embedded in my bones and likely to be, yea even unto time's end. Some distant day, in some other-where, a husband would cry pettishly that he simply didn't understand me. And the poor fellow would be right. For how could he, never having known the smell of fouled ditches nor witnessed our watery distances dissolving into darkness? (To this day I feel uneasy in Beauty Spots.)

We slogged on through puddles and pools between an avenue of glum specials, doubtlessly marvelling at this manifestation of what can happen to people who pass A-levels and confirmed in a long held belief that learning actually *does* soften the brain.

A small aeroplane now busied itself, dragging a string of huge capitals – *GO HOME RECIDIVISTS*. "How encouraging!" the Vicar remarked. "How very encouraging! There's hope yet for Old England when Young Farmers' Clubs not only know what that means but can spell it." But this hostile message from the heavens was too much for an old lady ahead of us because she broke ranks, splashed through a half-filled ditch and flung herself at the chain-link fence. "Murderers!" she screeched in cultivated tones. I admiringly supposed that she was about to bite her way onto American soil but she was only gnashing her teeth, and a young fellow, well protected in a riding mac, leapt after her and gently led her back to the road.

"Promise that you won't tell your father, Tom," she gasped. Thank goodness no one here knows us."

And that was about all which happened. The Yanks had been stored away into bunkers with their missiles and had left a front of our own countrymen who disarmed us by cheerily calling everyone over forty 'Gran' or 'Grandpa' and by handing out plastic fertilizer sacks to protect us from our ancient common foe. In fact, the forces of order and disorder became so indistinguishably soaked that, by the time somebody blew a whistle and we turned for home, a police inspector told the Vicar that he couldn't have asked for a nicer lot of protesters and wasn't it jolly good to be living in a Britain where there could be friendly exchanges of opinion on wet Saturday afternoons? But secretly I had hoped to redeem family honour by letting Miss Braceburn see that one Birtwisle heart beat in the right place. But this was not to be. Neither she nor Mustafa would so cravenly have surrendered to the downpour and I knew that, ahead, blocking Tyranny's Main Gate, one dauntless pair would be lying in the mud.

Mariana in her moated grange

To establish an alibi, I called at Polly's house or, as she insisted on naming herself and it since exposure to Lord

Tennyson's verses at too early an age, Mariana's Grange. Her mother had died bringing her into the world and her pa, having taken his broken heart off to Australia (where his ship struck a rock), she lived with her aged grandfather, Major Horbling.

I found her sprawled and overflowing his armchair, *Alfred Tennyson, a Selection,* on her lap and with TV and the radio full on. And when I reminded her that the set A-Level poet was Robert Browning, she snapped Yes and didn't she know it. "No heart, all head," she went on pettishly. "Even his name puts me off. Brings quick-mix gravy to mind. I even find Polly 'Horbling' less loathsome."

As she was saying this, she casually closed the book. Too late. I had spotted that she had been mooning over *Sir Galahad.* "You should eliminate Ronnie from your life," I advised her. "Surely you can see that he's utterly hopeless."

"He may be hopeless," she moaned. "But that doesn't make me less crazy about the gorgeous hunk. When he turns those big blue eyes on me, I melt down here." And she touched her upper jeans. "He is It. Oh, how I should like to spend some time in his arms."

I asked if a whiff of his armpits after PE had ever drifted her way and expressed doubt that she could survive overlong a session. She may not have heard me. "Hetty, what do you suppose it's like," she went on. "I mean being wrapped in a man's arms all night. All snug and delish and not leaping at each little sound outside the door. I feel that sort of thing may be my raison d'etre – if you follow me."

And she put on her swooningly distracted look and pushed her pudgy fingers through her unnaturally blonde locks. I directed her attention to the Major's cavalry sabre hanging menacingly above the fireplace and added, "I don't believe Ronnie would be up to it. 'Galahad' suits him to a T."

"Oh, you will see nothing good in him," she cried. "Ever

9

since la Braceburn has had us for Eng. Lit. you've got her and Browning on the brain."

"There simply is no comparison between Robert Browning's Childe Roland and Alf Tennyson's Galahad," I said coldly.

"Oh rubbish!" she objected huffily. "What about

> 'His tough lance thrusteth sure.
> His strength is as the strength of ten
> Because his heart is pure.'"

"Pooh! Queen Victoria must have given the old boot-licker the nod that if he kept her own Galahad, Albert, uppermost in his poor mind, she would see he made the peerage."

All the same I felt that I was being rather harsh, for Ronnie was quite handsome in a flaccid sort of way. By that I mean that, although most of his parts were beyond reproach – golden hair with a crinkle, wedgwood blue eyes, resolute chin, narrow waist, long legs – these did not add up to a heartstopping whole. Something was missing. You looked and knew that it was not in him to run off with a child-bride (as did Shelley) or chase Guinevere instead of the Holy Grail.

But Mariana was quite worked up and crushed me with, "And why do you have to talk like a book?"

"I suppose it must be what Latin has done to me," I said feebly. "Taking it to university entrance standard I mean. But I really do try."

But she would not be soothed.

"I suppose you can't help being overgrown, skinny and generally drab; after all, it isn't your doing that your Mum's meals must always be as mingy as when I last came to supper in Year Dot. And didn't she go on about that teeth-jarring spare-rib and what a butcher's bargain it was ('Wasn't it Dad?'). Does she always go on like that? I can't say you take after her, let alone him. What about your grandmammas?

You must have caught that red hair and flat chest from some-one. Doesn't it drive you crazy not having big boobs like that Ruben's Juno in Miss Witherpen's art-room? Or me?"

I replied scornfully that I was well satisfied with things as they were and would not want it put about that each day I was re-inflated by a bicycle pump. And (fearing further acrimony) I added that it was high time I hurried home if I was to be spared the Inquisition.

"Grandpa's on a route march," she called after me. "If you run into each other, please don't keep him nattering; it's time the stew left the oven. Try to make him understand that the runner-beans have gone into the pan. That'll hasten his stumbling tread."

As I walked quickly on my way, I felt that life must have more in store than being parcelled nightly into a man's arms for fifty faithful years, dishing up three meals daily and, next morning, it starting all over again. Or, if I escaped matri-mony, being offered around like a gift-wrapped doll with big boobs. Such a life-prospect was appalling.

By this time I had reached the Forty Foot and espied the Major helm down in the teeth of an easterly gale, his tweed hat dragged down over his ears and fighting a way along the further bank. He stumped onto the bridge and we cowered in its lee.

"What must I do, Major," I yelled, "for a happy life. But not over-happy? To fulfil myself?"

"Eh?" he shouted.

"Advice!" I screamed. "I need some advice. I want a rewarding life!"

"Marry a good man," he shouted back. "A religious man! A good man!"

"I don't have marriage in mind, Major. Anyway, not for some years. For the time being I just want to explore my potential. Fulfil my promise! If you follow me. And Polly

11

says the beans are in the pan."

"Marry a good man, Hetty," he cried. "A God-fearing man brought up by devout parents in the Church of England.

A confirmed man! Tending towards High Church practices! A man who keeps a Bible at his bedside. A good man!" And he waved his stick and stumped off, bending his body to the gale.

By this time the Peace-marchers had withdrawn to more hospitable climes and Jordans Bank had resumed its normal mantle — a settlement knocked up from back-wall bricks bought cheap when a brickyard went bankrupt, the occasional discouraged tree and half-a-dozen farmhouses sinking into the peat. I could not bring myself to dislike the place. It was all that I ever had known because, although Dad owned an elderly Morris Minor, he had set his face against journeying beyond Peterborough in one direction and Wisbech in the other. So all I knew about Beyond was from novels and the Major and Mariana's TV. (He had set his face against that also.)

As I passed the pub I spied a recent postscript, *WARMONGERS WELCOMED,* to the landlord's permanent slogan, *NO PEACE CAMPERS SERVED,* and paused to examine a postcard some silly wit from Away had pinned beneath the electric bell,

PRESS THIS FOR A FREE TEN
MINUTE TALK BY MRS THATCHER

Then I spurted forward once more and, noting the carnage in the greenhouse, congratulated myself on not telling Mariana how I had spent the afternoon: she was inclined to garrulous indiscretion.

Miss Braceburn

Mariana and I were luminaries of Waterland High, an establishment absentmindedly spared dread comprehensivisation. Its head was Mr. F. Spendlow, B.Sc., who had spent his life in educational institutions since that long-gone morning when his mother had trundled him into one, doubtlessly kicking and screaming, foreseeing the long sentence he was about to serve. He was now harmlessly institutionalised and forgettable.

The staff, by and large, were a lacklustre lot. Most had been laid to rest there for so long that they walked and talked like zombies, uttering such dreary slogans as 'Take down these notes I took down thirty years ago', 'Now where did we leave off last time?' or 'Girls, we must ready ourselves for the dawning Technological Age.' Now and then one disappeared or, reaching sixty-five, was put out to pasture with an inscribed clock to mark the unforgiving years. And these were replaced by restless young women on the look-out for socially suitable husbands but, finding only rugger club drunks or bank clerks dedicated to the care of aged mothers, worked out their year and moved on.

For the life of me I could not imagine how Miss Braceburn had come to rest there. She plainly had known better days; in fact, she revealed that she had known Philip Larkin as 'Phil' and, at a literary lunch, had lightly turned a jest with Stevie Smith. And those luminaries whom she could never have known because they already were dead − her astonishing assertions detailing domestic indiscretions were so convincing that we were ready to believe that she must have known them, perhaps in some already lived life.

For, once launched upon the deep, she must have had them spinning in their graves and likely to burst out. Even dreary old Matthew Arnold —

> " 'Ah love!" (she would moan) " 'Let us be true
>   To one another. . . .' "

and really she would seem to be in deep distress, pressing bony knuckles to her ribs and gasping,

> " '. . . for the world which seems
>   To lie before us like a land of dreams
>   Hath neither joy nor light nor help from pain.' "

Mariana and I discussed this phenomenon. "The dumplings," she declared. "When I dish them warmed-up for supper, Grandpa groans also. But *he* needs no more than a single Settler tablet to steady him."

Although this was absurd, I did not contest it. Because Miss B had hope that I might snatch the rare Oxbridge scholarship for Waterland High, she gave me extra coaching. Thus we were well enough acquainted for me to know her for what she was — a sea-green incorruptible. She had been born one, was one and would die one. For her, Eng. Lit. was not livelihood; it was life. And a session with her might go something like this.

"Hetty, what is your opinion of Robert Browning? A critical and considered judgment please. Robert Browning — the man not the reputation?"

"Oh," (I might say), "That is easily answered, Miss Braceburn. The past year with him has been an absolute revelation. From now on I measure all other men against him. There certainly is no one remotely like him in the Upper Sixth. This, of course, is a personal and perhaps minority opinion; it is not shared by at least one who could be mentioned."

14

"Please do not," she might reply. "But Hetty, promise that you will be more discriminating in your use of adjectives. Always ask if they do or do not enhance the value of a statement. For instance, would not 'revelation' alone be enough? And the word, 'absolute' — I should like you to look up what the Shorter Oxford has to say on 'absolute'. It is unstable, a word to be handled with extremest caution.

"However, you are right about Robert Browning: he is a free spirit. Since Cambridge days, he has been all to me. In looks (but for the hair which was of a reddish tinge similar to yours, Hetty), my tutor, Professor Massinger closely resembled early portraits of the poet. How he read verse! One felt that it might be R.B. himself. Like me, like you Hetty, Professor Massinger was an intellectual, a literary person. ('Literary' nota bene as distinct from 'literate'). Now let us look at *Abt Vogler, a Soliloquy*. Page 167

'All we have wished and hoped and dreamed of good
Shall exist. . . .'

(Never, never forget that, Hetty dear — even in, especially in moments of despair,)

'The passion that left the ground to lose itself in the sky
Is music sent up to God by the lover and the bard.
Enough that we heard it once: we shall hear it by and by.'

"And note the colon, a most misused mark of punctuation. Here we seen an exemplary use — indicating an abrupt corollary to a preceding statement.

"But Robert Browning is not for the light-minded." (Could she possibly have overheard my conversation with Mariana?) "Browning is for the strong, the resolute, for those eager to grapple with life. And with him! Particularly (now A-levels are upon us) with him!

"Recall *Vogler*. It is one of Robert Browning's truly great works. Like Beethoven's late quartets, like Goya in his so-called mad old age. Like William Shakespeare coming to his peak with *Lear*. Now – page 168 and lines 19 and 20. Consider that final cadence.

> 'Which I have dared and done, for my resting place is found –
> The C-Major of this life . . .'

" 'Hope! Cling to hope,' that is R.B.'s assertion in his *Abt Vogler*. He is saying, 'When hope is lost, all is lost.' Momentarily to digress – Promise me that (in a general way) you will cling to hope, Hetty."

"Oh yes, oh certainly, Miss Braceburn. "I will, I will. And (if at all possible) in C-Major."

"Not 'will'. The 1st Person Singular of the verb 'to be', Present Tense, is 'shall'. Perhaps you should cling to that also: your A-levels are only a few days distant."

That is how a session with Miss B might go.

Now back to actuality . . .

"Hetty," she said, "The other day at Jordans Bank . . . that gentleman . . . your father?"

I admitted this.

"Ah!" she said. "Ah yes! Now do remind me – what is Mr Birtwisle's occupation?"

I told her that he was a finance manager.

Despite her preoccupation with the poets, she was shrewd enough to know that this was untrue; a clutch of ball-points clipped into his breast pocket had betrayed him as rate-collector.

"Is your dawg recovered from Saturday's downpour?" I asked. "And how did he get his unusual name?"

"Oh, he is quite well, thank you, Hetty," she replied, smiling. "He is not a sensitive dawg; he has a sound constitution and does not harbour grudges. And yes . . . his name? Mustafa was that Turkish-gun-dog in some war or other, who, his battery's crew dead or dying, snatched in his

16

teeth a fiery brand and (so we are told) touched off the loaded cannon's fuse to cut a swathe in the ranks of the advancing French (a degenerate race). When I return to my flat this evening, I shall tell him of your enquiry."

She then looked long and speculatively at me, swept up books and gown, and loped off. And, for at least ten minutes afterwards, I knew that all we dreamed of good would exist, that virtue would triumph in the end. And that my day would come.

On our homeward bus I took this up with Mariana who, despite approaching A-levels, was sex-obsessed. "But do you not recognize Browning's intellectual superiority to Tennyson, one with little but frustrated sensual inclinations on his poor mind? I ask without rancour; after all his engagement to Emily Sellwood lasted sixteen years and he was a man who ate well."

"Not sex," she replied, gazing devotedly at Ronnie's golden head along the gangway. "Love!"

"From non-syllabus holiday-reading, I have always supposed that men look upon the two as one and the same," I countered. "When they go on about heart, it is bosoms or bottoms they have in mind."

"And, what of it?" she said crudely. "I rather like them fancying my knockers. I say, do you remember Miss Livesay dissecting that bull's heart she'd scrounged from the butcher's and those two nearest her demonstration bench fainting and Lucy Gill spewing-up? And anyway, I bet Lord Tennyson wouldn't have sloped off on the sly with Liz Barratt. He would have charged down Wimpole Street and kicked down the front door and tied her ghastly father to the bannisters with his own braces."

"Whatever has the bull's heart and Lucy Gill to do with that?" I asked irritably. But she was in a tizzy, Ronnie having turned and graciously acknowledged our being alive. So I

17

didn't contest the ridiculous supposition. Sadly our literary heritage was wasted on Mariana. She was a jolly good sort, an ever-present help in time of trouble but had this coarse streak, quite unlike her grandfather, the Major, who, despite his warlike preoccupations, was a man of some sensibility.

(Nevertheless I decided against telling her that, as we left the dining-hall, Ronnie had pushed his big hot hand at me and muttered, Would I meet him at the Saturday disco in his Dad's churchroom?)

"Are you going to the disco?" Mariana asked.

"You know very well it would be hopeless. Dad would only ask where the fifty pence was to come from and provide an opportunity for him to hint that I would spend the evening in the bushes and come home with a baby inside me."

"God, I hope you land that university scholarship and escape," she lamented. "These are the best years of your life and look what's happening to them. If you don't get good enough grades, what do you suppose will happen to you?"

"I don't know," I replied. "Although I suspect that Dad does, so I expect I shall end up in the council-offices."

"Do you think men have any part in Miss B's life?" Mariana asked, yet again irritatingly tripping our conversation to its flip side.

"She must have had a father."

"You know very well what I mean," she insisted. "Some time or other even she must have fired a spark in some chap's breast. When one looks around it's staggering what some men can fancy. Amazingly, there really does seem to be somebody for everybody. Besides, how can she go on so about love, if she's never had any?"

"Perhaps her sweetheart was killed in the War," I suggested (having heard this frequently advanced as a reason for celibacy).

"Which war?" she cried scornfully. "There hasn't been a proper one for donkeys years."

But I was feeling vaguely disloyal discussing Miss B behind her back and drew her attention to a lone figure hunched on a grassy bank and gazing into the dyke.

"It's only Daft Dick," she said dismissively. "He's not interested in girls: only in eels. They say he dives in and catches them with his teeth, then devours them raw."

The bus stopped by our sub-post office stores. And so we parted and I loitered Osokosie-wards, still puzzled why Miss Livesay's dissection of a bull's heart had anything to do with either Alfred Tennyson or Robert Browning or, for that matter, Miss Braceburn's lost lover.

The Trouble with John Donne

I felt sick the instant that I opened the living-room door. Storm clouds had gathered and the air was crackling with undischarged venom. Sonny, his protruding grey eyes shining and his antennae revolving happily, was pretending to glue together an airfix bomber he had finished a week ago; Mum was dropping purls like mad and had face-twitch. I avoided looking at Dad and made for the staircase, hearing myself say shakily, "Hello everyone. I shall get on with my swotting right away. Not hungry, Mum; we had dumplings with both courses today."

"Come back," he ordered.

So I had to look. He was rubbing up his bristly little moustache and tapping a knee (a certain warning of eruption). Mum sidled off into the kitchen, muttering about a smell of burning. Sonny gave up fiddling and looked even happier when ordered to bring back Mum. "Tell her that I want her here no matter what she's doing," he was told. "This filthy business has got to be fetched out into the open. And tell her, Now. This minute!"

Then he turned on me.

"What's this, Miss, I found concealed under the bolster in your bedroom?" he demanded, topping up his rage with a 'What's this, What's this?' "Yes, it's you, Miss Clever, I'm talking to. Yes, you!"

And dramatically he turned an opened book towards me. It was my John Donne.

"Oh so this is the foul muck you gloat over up there," he shouted. "In your bed, I suppose. In your bed! Gloat over it in your bed eh! And don't bother putting on that innocent look. You know what I'm on about, you shameless creature."

He put on his reading spectacles.

" 'License my roving hands. . . .' Pah! I won't soil my lips with the filth."

"It's a school text-book, dad," I explained feebly. "Mr Spendlow, the Headmaster, issues them from his stockroom. I need it for my A-levels next week. I wasn't hiding it. I was studying just before I turned off the light; that's why it was beneath the bolster. I have to read it so that I can answer the General Section questions they set. And the man who wrote it was Dean of St Paul's Cathedral and I believe that he's buried there."

That flummoxed him. He was so enraged that he half rose to hit me but, instead, hurled the text-book. It missed me and brought down the second pot duck flying across the wallpaper. This shattered.

Mum was all of a twitter. She began to whimper.

"Go on up to your room," he yelled. "No supper for her, Grace. Definitely no supper for her. And take it out of her dinner-money till that duck's paid for."

20

He fired a last shot as I was halfway up the stairs. "And you're not to play that blasted gramophone of yours." (Sonny must have found that well worthwhile waiting for; he coveted it.)

This ancient wind-up artefact, superannuated by Mariana, was parked on the varnished chest-of-drawers along with my library of seventeen records, chiefly 78s. They were a mixed bunch picked up at bring-and-buy sales and ranged from Fats Waller to William Byrd's Mass for Five Voices. Only my Françoise Hardy ('Tous les garcons et les filles amoureuses') had been bought new. They were my revival kit when spirits sagged, when (as poor Tennyson says)

> . . . the nerves prick
> And tingle and the heart is sick
> And all the wheels of being slow.

Music being denied me, I sought consolation from my picture, a print from a colour supplement showing Matthew Arnold's Scholar Gypsy cowering to peer over a rural bridge's parapet extraordinarily like our own Forty-Footer — and in a snow storm. Until that evening it had not occurred to me that perhaps he was wondering whether to jump and have done with things. This brought on a fit of introspective gloom. I had long known that Dad did not love me and now I was all but sure that he actively disliked me and may always have done so. I was not unduly cast down by this revelation: after all I had survived eighteen years and, if A-levels went well, deliverance was at hand.

So I drew up a chair to my rickety table and looked across the lane towards the distant vicarage moored in its watery wastes. Ronnie must have bolted supper because, as though on cue, he emerged, energetically pedalling; it was Choir Practice evening and he played the organ. Alas, Mariana, I mourned,

> For leagues no other tree did mark
> The level wastes, the rounding grey . . .

and now, here was her Galahad cantering off. But to where? Not to the Grange. That lay in the opposite direction. Alas, alas!

> 'She only said, 'My life is dreary,
> He cometh not,' she said. . . .'

And I thought smugly, she has not my intellectual resources to fall back upon. Poor Mariana! Poor Polly! This reminded me to explore my satchel and to make a last effort to plumb the murkier depths of Browning's thinking as unrevealed to me in *Abt Vogler,* who could be relied upon to come up in A-levels so that (as Miss Braceburn declared) examiners might sound depths and chart shallows. But yet again his message eluded me and yet again I falsely fell back upon learning by heart a clutch of suitable lines to screen my ignorance.

However, after a couple of hours of this intellectual exercise, I felt quite myself once more, subduing even self-reproach for neglecting to cache a few biscuits to tide me over just such an emergency. Yet, even so, I knew that it was not enough merely to survive tyranny; one must strike a blow for freedom. So I took out the pink notepaper and matching envelopes Mum had given me for Christmas and put pen to paper,

To the Editor, Waterland Weekly Messenger,

Sir,
    May I through the hospitality of your columns venture to protest against the hostility shown to the Nuclear Protesters by the Authorities and by the General Public of Jordans Bank. In such a fashion did not the citizens of Bethlehem receive the Holy Child in a bleak midwinter long ago? . . .

Then I sat back and examined the house-stabilizer which

passed across my room. (Stabilizers are the steel rods clamped to outer walls which prevent fenland houses falling apart.) There was scratching on the window-pane and it was Percy, a black tomcat basely cast adrift when his family had flitted. On rough nights or in his rare moods of depression, he scaled the scullery's sloping roof and sought shelter under my bed. He was an extremely perceptive animal who, understanding my circumstances, knew that any exchange of greeting might give the game away. So I pushed up the sash and he stealthily slipped in.

I felt quite calm by this time and, feeling that, from an unusually unpromising start the evening had recovered itself, slept well.

A Final Test

By Fenland standards, the morning of my A-levels final exam dawned bright and propitious so, ignoring Ronnie's brushing past me more intimately than was warranted as he stumbled up the bus gangway, I reluctantly paid attention to Mariana who was saying that, on such a morning (although an evening and, more particularly, an autumn evening would have her preference), she would not mind dying like *your* Browning's *Evelyn Hope.* "It would be super to know that Ronnie might sit by my bedside, bitterly regret earlier inattention to my charms and, before withdrawing, press a flower into my hand. After all, *your* Browning's Evelyn was only sixteen. Being paler, as I suppose I should be, would make me look quite brill, don't you suppose, Hetty?"

"But there is no evidence in the poem that she wanted to die," I objected. "I imagine that it was consumption brought on by dowsing her tea and rice puddings with nontubercular tested milk. But, yes, I do see what you mean. And, in the event, you can rely on me."

"You mean that you'd die too?" she asked naively. "Thanks a lot, Hett."

"I mean that I would sit by you for old time's sake," I said. "I have never seen a corpse but imagine that I shouldn't mind yours too much."

(A yellow dredger was scooping up weeds and sludge from a distant dyke.)

She can't have heard this because she went on, "Yes, Ronnie knowing all of a sudden as I lay there that, in his heart of hearts, he'd loved me all the time. . . ." And she mournfully recited,

> Beautiful Evelyn Hope is dead,
> Sit and watch by her side an hour.
> This is her bookshelf, this her bed.
> She plucked this piece of geranium flower.

"You might repent the impulse," I remarked. "Once gone, you can't change your mind, you know. I scarcely believe it would be worthwhile going through with and afterwards putting your Grandpa to heavy funeral expense just to have Ronnie stop-by on his way to play tennis with Lucy Gill. And are you not afraid that an examination of your bookshelf might give him the impression of a light mind?"

It was the mention of Lucy, whom she loathed, which brought her back to earth.

"I suppose so," she said, admitting both likelihoods and glaring bitterly at the back of Galahad's head. "After all, I suppose if she (and I am not referring to that Gill creature) had stuck it out until she was seventeen or eighteen and like the pair of us in the Upper Sixth, she might have got over her crush."

"The poem does not say that she had a crush," I objected

24

reasonably enough. "I imagine that she was no more than a sex-symbol in his eyes and he was feasting them on her for a last time before going on to Another One."

"Oh, let's leave it," Mariana said crossly. "Did you look at last night's Dallas?"

"You know we haven't TV. Anyway I was having a last look at Robert Browning."

"Oh blast Browning!" she cried. "The old bore! Agonizing away like mad: I suppose la Braceburn takes him to bed with her. Thank God for *Gidner's Textual Interpretations*. With his support, Browning and her can waffle on until they're blue in their face."

(With my approaching two hours ordeal in mind, I mentally substituted 'she' and 'faces'.)

"It's good old *Gidner*'ll drag me through if anyone can. There's not an examiner born who can think up questions Gidner hasn't thought up first – and written model answers for. You should have taken my advice, Hetty and borrowed my copy."

"Let some dusty old pen-pusher think for me!" I protested "Even if he could (which he can't), it would be beneath scorn. I hope for an examiner who recognizes and rewards the opinions of an independent mind when they are pushed under his nose."

But now we had reached Waterland High and alighted to face the day.

Actually, when I took my place in the gym and opened the set paper, I found myself able to examine the questions with a decent composure, settling on no. 2 to open my innings. This was,

> *'In your opinion, which major poem demonstrates Browning's assertion that Life is but a prelude to the Greater Theme of Eternity? Discuss.'*

And, only after pondering this for some minutes (for Miss B so often had cautioned us against rushing into panic-stricken scribble) did I firmly announce my intention,

' "All we have wished and hoped and dreamed of good shall exist.
The passion that left the ground to lose itself in the sky
Are music sent up to God by the lover. . . ." '

(and here and momentarily, thought strayed wilfully to Mariana)

'. . . and the bard.'

And this done, I wandered off into delicate nuances of speculation and variations on my theme —

'Thus (I wrote) the old capelmeister, Abt Vogler, as the empty church darkened. . . .'

And well and truly launched and with a fair and following wind, I wrote on and on convincingly. Well, anyway, it convinced *me*.

Outside, I half-heard the usual four o'clock row as the lowing herd departed. Then the bleak stillness of a school abandoned to its cleaning ladies. And finally, at a bell's ping, I rose and walked stiffly into the corridor, knowing that I had given my all for Waterland High, for Miss Braceburn and for Robert Browning. So that it was with anti-climactic misgiving that I saw Ronnie, that knight without stain, waiting for me at the foot of the staircase. To put it mildly, with R.B. still frothing in my head, to be reminded of Alf Tennyson was crushing. For, although I had never heard Ronnie at the organ, I felt pretty sure that he was not in the same street as Abt Vogler (particularly in C-Major).

"We can just about catch that second bus," he muttered. "Did you get my note? And here's some pinks I picked in our garden. Oh and old Bracebones asked me to give you this."

Hetty dear,

I read yr letter to the Weekly Messenger and, whilst
applauding yr sentiments which do you credit, I was appalled at the
extravagant style in which they were expressed . . .

Good heavens, I had utterly forgotten that letter and, with
this ominous news coming on the heels of exam hangover,
Ronnie might as well have caught the 4.30 and tried his luck
with Mariana.

"I meant it, Hetty," he muttered as we alighted at Sickert's
Corner.

"Meant what?" I asked sharply, still preoccupied.

He looked past my shoulder. "I meant what I said in the
note. That I'd fallen for you in a big way. Dad wants me to
carry on to theological college but I'd rather go off with you.
You know."

"I know what?"

"You know!"

"No, I don't," I snapped. "For goodness sake stop shilly-
shallying and tell me."

"We could be lovers," he said, going a brightish red, "and
go off to – well, go to Australia say. Or New Zealand, though
that would cost more."

"Thank you, Ronnie," I said abstractedly. "Perhaps some
other time. . . ."

Striking a blow for Freedom

As I entered I knew immediately that I was in for another
pulsating drama of the Wild East. The same scenario as
before but with the *Weekly Messenger* standing in for John
Donne. The same stage-set, the same cast – Mum knitting
hopelessly, Sonny busying himself with a jig-saw and

pulsing big bursts of joy.

The principal performer was fretting centre-stage, impatiently waiting for me to walk-on.

"Did you write this?" he raged, slapping a folded newspaper at his thigh. "Did you? And don't lie. You did. I can see that you did from your brazen face."

"And my signature too, I suppose," I shakily managed to get out.

"You have dragged me in the mud," he shouted. "And not just me! Us all! And not just in front of the neighbours! At my place of business! In front of the workmen. And the other council officers. And the councillors. Who do you think you are to question what is right and wrong? You look down on us, don't you? Don't deny it. Don't you dare deny it. You do. And you can cut out that fancy talk you've learned from those Horblings and talk ordinary, you blasted chit. You've had it over-soft that's what you've had; your mother and me had been out four years earning our living when we were your age and the sooner you get your stuck-up nose down to a real job the better, you young monkey." It burst from him like a flood.

He had so often declared himself disappointed, put out, insulted that, if I kept quiet, the storm blew itself out. This time was going to be different: he was set on working himself up to a towering rage.

"You idle, cheeky, good-for-nothing!" he shouted.

Mum set off for the kitchen to stop what was burning.

"Come back," he yelled. "I warned you it would come to this. But nothing could persuade you. You had to have your way. Now sit down."

She sat down.

"Well, what have you to say, you hard-faced hussy?"

"I shall go to my room, Dad," I faltered. "And I am sorry the letter offended you. I didn't mean it to."

"Don't you dare defy me," he cried, repeatedly bashing down the rolled newspaper on the table-top in hard sharp slaps. "Don't! Don't . . . you . . . dare."

I now knew that this was unlike anything which had happened before. He had been smouldering ever since the John Donne affair. Perhaps even before that – when Miss Braceburn bested him in the garden. This was eruption.

He leapt to his feet. And came at me.

I ran for it, leaping up the stairs two at a time and slammed my door. In vain.

"And now, you little bitch," he screamed. "And now I'm going to teach you a lesson you'll never forget. Not Now, not Tomorrow, not Never!" And gave me an almighty slap across the face. I dodged a second and, with my longer arms, fended him off, digging my fingers between his neck and shirt collar until a button flying off into my face so startled me that I lost my grip and, in a mad panic, began to half-strangle him with a two-handed twist on his tie. He was beside himself at this resistance and when (although not really meaning to) I hacked his shins, in between roars of pain and gulps for air, revealed a scabrous range of vocabulary which, in happier time, I might have admired, even modified my opinion of him as an ill-tempered, sanctimonious bully.

But meanwhile we heaved to and fro, bumping and bashing from my chest-of-drawers across to the further wall. Down went my wicker table and, as we fell, a leg cracked. (Oddly enough, in this bizarre extremity, I thought, If there's one thing that I cannot put up with, it's writing on a rickety table.) Next, my pile of records was swept to the floor and down we went too. And up again like indiarubber all-in wrestlers, hair all over my face, him slavering down his chin. He lunged, grabbed my waist, fox-trotted me towards the bed and, weight telling, twisted me till I collapsed across his knees, head dangling, legs kicking.

The brief but savage struggle was over.

He twitched up my gymslip and began smacking, accompanying each flat-hander with a single word – "You're . . . too . . . big . . . for . . . your . . . boots . . . madam. . . . Far . . . too . . . big. . . .

Slip round neck, one shoe gone, sobbing in frustrated rage . . . and he went on chanting breathlessly and whacking.

Then he let me slither to the lino and I heard the key turn in the lock.

After a time I scrambled up and lay shuddering on the bed. Shame. Fury. Not pain. And that is how I stayed, first hearing Sonny excitedly mounting to his room, then Mum who stopped at my door and only moved on when she heard him stirring below. I suppose that I must have slept because, hours later, I was aroused by his car going off.

I tried the door. It still was locked.

An Astonishing Revelation

So this, I thought, is what life is all about when one really gets down to the nitty-gritty. Not like Miss Braceburn's rhapsodies, not like Eng.lit. Well, better to learn early than late. Farewell Robert Browning.

So I said quite loudly, "That mush is dead and done with. Now let the heavens fall . . ."

And then, gulping back spasms of furious tears, I fell asleep again.

When I came-to, Mum was bleating quite piteously on the landing. "Oh do say something, Ethel. Only a word. Just one word to say you're OK. Did he hurt you much? I don't see why you should hold it against me. I've always done my best for you: he'd have taken you out of school two years ago if it

30

hadn't been for me. Oh do say something."

Then, after a pause and doubtlessly with her ear to the door's panels, "There are things I can't tell you about. Not yet anyway. About your Dad and me. To tell you the honest truth I'm a bit scared of him myself."

(A bit! I thought. That's a laugh.)

"He can be real unkind," she went on. " I could tell you things if only you were older. Butter wouldn't melt in his mouth when he was courting me. Back then I wasn't like I am now. I was only a twelvemonth older than you. Are you there, Ethel? It all seemed to start when the doctor told him we couldn't have any babies. Only he doesn't know I know that. Your Auntie Phyllis told me I ought to let on I knew who it was couldn't do it and that it wasn't me. But that would only have made him take it out on me."

(It took a little time for this astonishing information to sink in and I should have liked to have had it repeated.)

"Can you hear me, Ethel?" she called anxiously.

"Yes, of course I can," I hissed. "I am not lying in a pool of blood or hanging from the house-stabilizer tie-rod."

She unlocked the door.

"He doesn't know I've got this key," she said smugly. "And that's not the only thing he doesn't know. What did he do to you, dear?"

I told her.

"Oh!" she said. "So he did that, did he! Across his knees, eh? Oh he did!" And she nodded her head like a clockwork doll but with a far from dolly look on her puffy face.

"He didn't do anything else?" she asked anxiously. "Anything you don't like talking about? You're sure he only did what you told me he did?"

She began picking up smashed gramophone records. Then she said and perhaps to herself, "Now I understand something I noticed after he'd gone off to work when I did the washing. Well, who would have thought it! Well!" And she went over to the window, nodding mysteriously.

Then she turned back towards me and said, "You can't stay here now, dear. You've got to go. Right away and not come back. But promise you'll never let on it was me told you. Never! This isn't a fit place for you anymore. So long as you won't tell on me, I'll say you got out of the window and slid down the scullery roof. Like your cat."

"My cat?"

"Yes, that's the way it gets in and out, isn't it?"

"Oh so you know about him then?"

"I have a nose," she said. "And a mouth I can keep shut when you've gone away."

"Away?" I exclaimed. "Away to where? Where can I go? After all, this is my home."

She ignored this cri-de-coeur. In fact, I doubt if she heard me. Instead, she left the room and returned with a handful of money. "There's sixteen pound here. I put it by in drips and drabs out of the housekeeping," she purred (seeking approval for her cunning). "He never knew. You can have it to get your started. You can find lodgings somewhere. Then with all your education you'll easy get a job."

"Me! A job!"

"Well, you were going to get one whether you liked it or not. It's practically fixed up at the council offices for next week. They were going to put you on the switchboard."

"On a switchboard!"

"Here, take your kitbag and what you can't get into that, can go in this Finefare carrier."

All this time she was emptying drawers and cramming my wardrobe willynilly into the haversack I'd brought from Millet's Surplus. It was all quite bewildering but she couldn't have found a better way of taking my mind off things.

"Most of your records have got smashed," she mourned.

"And them that's not smashed look bent. The one I liked most was that foreign one. On the quiet I did used to enjoy it. I couldn't make out the words, of course. That foreign one, I mean. But all the same it made me think of before I was married, when I was a girl like you. The days when I used to lie in my bed of a morning and wonder what would become of me."

She brooded on this.

"I must say I never imagined anybody like your Dad."

She was yakking away like a zombie. "Oh do give me a hand," she fussed. "Sonny'll be back for his dinner." (She did not appear to understand that what she had told me through the door was boiling my head off.)

"Listen Mum," I said firmly, "And for goodness sake – that carrier-bag is splitting already. No, not that dress: I can't get into it anymore. Not the bag. The dress! That dress! Please do listen. Am I. . . . Did you say that I am not his daughter? That he is not my father?"

"How could you be?" And she smirked. "How could you be? Haven't I just told you what the doctor said? He can't be anybody's father."

"Was there another man then?"

"What other man?"

"Did you have me by another man?"

"Oh Ethel! Even if I did which I didn't, he'd have killed me."

"Then what about Sonny? Is he not my brother?"

"Of course not, silly. How could he be? We had him from a council refuge in Balham. You came from a posh nursing home in Birmingham. The matron said he'd been dumped on a police-station doorstep. He only had the few bits and pieces whoever she was left him in. Whereas you had two full sets of the best of everything. Not like him, poor little mite!"

This was breath-taking.

"Are you positive he didn't do anything else to you, dear?"

"Who?"

"Your Dad. Did he just spank you? Nothing else?"

I shook my head.

"You must have put up a fight," she said admiringly. "That red mark round his neck was still there when he went off to work, though he tried to cover it with his scarf. And he didn't half let out some terrible groans during the night. Did you kick him, dear?"

For a moment or two the poor dispirited woman went through some sort of spiritual struggle. In fact, it must have been quite a severe attack because, when she spoke, it was in tones of deep solemnity. "This is yours, Ethel." And she pushed a tight little packet of tissue paper towards me. It was a silver brooch, a circlet of flowers enclosing an absolutely glorious aquamarine. "The matron told me in confidence that *she* handed you over with it. What I mean is that it fastened the shawl you came in. He never saw it. He doesn't know I've had it all these years, which is a marvel because he's forever rummaging through my things when I'm out. (And he doesn't know that either.) Sonny came with nothing when they handed *him* over; only just what he'd been left in."

I felt enormously bucked at retrieving this charming and romantic fragment from my past. Like Miss Braceburn, I appeared to have known better days.

"Are you quite sure you don't know who I am?" I demanded.

"Of course I know. You're what you've always been – our Ethel."

"Who I really am! And please stop calling me 'Ethel': I hate it."

Seemingly it never had occurred to her that I had started

34

life as someone else.

"Oh no," she explained anxiously. "They keep that sort of thing a dead secret. It's as much as their job's worth to let on. Even when *he* asked, they wouldn't tell him. But he got it out of them you were from a very respectable home and your clothes as good as told me you were from a clean one. And I don't like Ethel either. But he would have you called after his auntie. I wanted to call you Marilyn."

When I did not comment, she looked disappointed; evidently the long ago episode had been the one really exciting thing which ever had happened to her. "Now that I've told you, you're bound to think you've come down in the world. But you've got to admit we've done our level best. Even he was fond of you when you were a toddler."

She waved at the little shelf of my books hanging from a cord above the dresser. "He made that in fretwork. He was at it all one winter. And he cut himself twice."

She looked rather hopelessly at me. "The second time there was blood everywhere. You should have seen it. One of his handkerchiefs still has the stain."

There did not seem to be any adequate response to this: I didn't even encourage my nobler self to surface when she added, "He's not all that nimble with his hands. You should have seen all that blood."

Once more there was an awkward silence.

"It was when you passed that eleven-plus that he seemed to alter," she said reflectively. "I put it down to him thinking you were getting beyond him when you came home talking in French. And it was about that time when you got to know those Horblings up at The Grange and started speaking what he calls lah-di-dah. He's queer that way; he never liked me being bigger than him. He wouldn't let me have high heels. But you've got to admit you do talk too grown-up, like a book."

35

"You said that you collected me in Birmingham?"

"Yes and I didn't like it a bit. Nothing but rattle and filth."

Mmmmm, I thought, so that is where I must begin looking – Birmingham. Birmingham? (It did not sound a propitious start in life.)

"Right!" I said. "I see that I cannot stay here if you mean what I believe you mean about your husband. So I shall seek my fortune elsewhere! A clerk! Did you say he had arranged for me to be a clerk. Well, not even a clerk! On a switchboard! The appalling cheek! But thank you for the money. Of course I shall return it to you when I have found employment. Don't be alarmed: he needn't know. I shall send it by way of Polly.

"And the brooch – thank you for keeping it for me; it will be a reminder that once I was someone else."

"Wherever will you go, Ethel?"

"Where Dick Whittington went, I suppose," I replied quite airily. "London! In books, outcasts always end up there. I never recall reading of anyone seeking her fortune in Stoke-on-Trent."

"Oh dear!" she wailed. "I don't like to see you having to go off like this. You're that young. And I was so looking forward to your Wedding Day. I was going to have a new coat and a hat and shoes. And maybe one of those handbags you can't tell from leather. That's what the sixteen pound was the start of."

I opened the window and arranged sketchy evidence of flight. Then I wound up my gramophone and put on Francoise Hardy, although it was deeply scratched and done for. Before she locked the door, I took a last look around my refuge and, even on the landing, could not drag myself away.

"Come on." she said impatiently. "Why are you stood there? What are you listening to? I can't hear anything. Only that gramophone. There's nobody in there now."

36

"I am not there anymore," I said.

"Of course you're not. How can you be? You're here on the landing."

Oh dear, it was so sad. There would be the chest, the bookshelf, the bed, a pile of ruined records, a rickety table. But not me.

We went downstairs and outside. As I turned away up the cinder-path she called quaveringly, "It's funny, Ethel: that's about the only time you and me have had a grown-up talk. And that's another thing he's taken away from me. It'll never happen now: I mean coming round to your house to have my tea on a Sunday after you were married. And going over the week with you. And maybe later, being a granny. . . . But wasn't it funny when he missed you and hit that daft duck?"

Fancy, I thought, I have stopped thinking of the poor creature as 'Mum' already. Yet she nursed me and bathed me and wheeled me out and showed me off. And worried when I was ill. . . . So I turned in my tracks. Big tears were rolling down her puffy cheeks and she ran towards me and we kissed.

Then I headed for the railway station still hearing the ruined record fretfully repeating again and again from an empty room,

> Tous les garcons et les filles amoureuses,
> Tous les garcons et les filles de mon âge . . .

"Well, I am not the first," I said loudly (to bolster confidence). "There was Dick Whittington and his cat. En avant!"

I looked around me: there was no sign of Percy.

Nevertheless, having had it sprung upon me that I did not belong to any readily available body was, to say the least, novel. It happens. I have read of it happening. But it does not happen often. And it had never happened to me. It had been my custom to plan not only for each day but for each week also and then for the month, even the year. I usually knew where I should be, who else would be there, where that night I should lay my head (although it must be admitted this always had been the same place. And now . . .

So I had to admit that the prospect before me was pretty cheerless and any port in a storm was called for. And along came Ronnie pedalling merrily away on his bike, to spring rather dashingly from it. "Why are you not at school?" I asked.

"I might ask you the same," he countered. "Can I come with you? Where are you going?"

"Away," I answered fairly off-handedly. "Penniless and friendless, I'm going off into the wide world to seek my fortune." And I held up the bulging Finefare bag and patted the haversack.

"You're joking, Hetty," he said, stooping to remove his bicycle clips.

"Ronnie," I went on, examining him with a lively eye, "Ronnie, I don't want to be bothersome, but you may recall suggesting that we went off together. I have considered your proposal and, in the prevailing circumstances, consent. How are we for cash? I can contribute sixteen pounds."

"Go off! Do you mean leave home? Go away for keeps? (His voice was rather shrill.) Wherever to?"

"I had London in mind. That is where runaways usually go and, as it happens, there is a train for Wisbech in about one hour – just time for you to hurry off to the Vicarage and grab necessities for life on the run."

He laughed uneasily and, manoeuvring me behind an elderberry bush, took me in his arms.

"Look," I said, wriggling from the hug and taking deep breaths of air, "I'm not joking, Ronnie. How much is there in your piggy-bank? There will be the train-fare and later I shall need some supper. Then we shall have to sleep somewhere.

You said that you wanted me. Well, here I am. All yours! And I shall stretch a point; you needn't marry me . . . anyway not for the time being."

(I delivered this by no means as bravely as it may sound.) He did not say 'No' at once; that much may be said for him. But he was manning his defences.

"Oh!" he said ruefully, "I believe you mean it. Oh, what a bore; we're off on our hols on Monday." (And blushed at the lie.) "But for that I'd love to have come. But Mummy has been absolutely weeks and weeks fixing things up and she'd be terribly miffed if I backed out at short notice. Booking you know and so on. . . . That sort of thing. Otherwise, as I say. . . ." His dreary refusal trailed away into his shoes.

"That's OK, Ronnie," I said, trying to sound as though I'd suggested a date at a disco. "Yes, I can see that it would be difficult, so I shall have to go without you."

"Perhaps, another time," he said, eagerly snatching the proffered get-out. "When I get back from Frinton we could discuss it again." And tried to grab me. "And you haven't told me why you are going (that is, if you do go). You'll probably be offered a place at a teachers' training college when A-levels come out. If you really do mean that you're off, promise that you'll write."

"Write? No, I think not."

"Oh, why not? I'd write back."

Poor Ronnie! He was pretty feeble.

"Ronnie," I said, "Do you recall that man who came by night?"

"No. Which man?"

"We had him in R.E. The one in Luke I believe."

"Oh him! But he went away again, didn't he?"

"Yes," I said, "He went away again. I seem to recall that the words were 'For he had great possessions.' "

"Well, what's that to do with it?"

I raised my eyes heavenward. And went. I knew that it wasn't fair but someone else had to be hurt. So I looked back; he still stood by the bush looking puzzled. "Farewell Galahad," I called bitterly. "That lance of yours – keep it sharp and shining. You never can tell when the next maiden-in-distress might come along."

"Who?" he shouted uncertainly. "Who? 'Galahad'! Did you say 'Galahad'? Who's Galahad? And my what?"

After the Battle

About now it began to rain. This weakened my resolve to shake Jordans Bank dust from my feet and I turned along the unkempt drive to The Grange. The Major, being deaf, knocking was in vain so I went straight in and found him poring over bound copies of *The Illustrated London News,* his finger tracing an illustrated account of the Battle of Majuba Hill. I touched his shoulder.

"Not like my War, Hetty. Not like our do. Oh no, not at all. Good heavens, No!" he shouted, tapping a steel engraving of redcoats dodging from boulder to boulder. "Fellow in the village – George Booms. Roadsweeper . . . remember him? Don't employ 'em nowadays, Hetty. Roadsweepers. Gadgets for every honest job. Is there any wonder chaps can't find work. Poor Booms – dead and gone now I daresay. Went out to Natal with the County Yeomanry, CO was old Colonel Bosanquet up at the Hall. Raised a battalion. That's gone too. The hall. And the battalion. And the Bosanquets. Only one of 'em left. Place in Northamptonshire, I'm told. Chaps with their heads well down. Pinned down by accurate musketry, y'see, Hetty. Booms says the old Colonel gets fretful. Did his soldiering out in India y'see. Bosanquet not Booms.

Maharatta Wars! Line advance out there! Present arms! Shoulder arms! Fire! That's our trouble, Hetty — always fighting the last war at the start of the next one."

(It was important to concentrate one's attention when the Major launched into a discursive account of battles lost and won in days of yore.)

"Booms says Bosanquet draws his sword, jumps up, yells, 'Forward men!' And they yell back, 'Get down quick, you silly old b*****.' And that he did, he did, by Gad. By Gad, he did that. Booms swears he'll remember till his dying day, 'Forward men!' tailing off into a gurgle. Boers got him in the throat, y'see Hetty. Then he went stone deaf."

"I should have supposed that it might have been very much worse, Major," I cried.

"Booms!" he shouted back. "It was George Booms the roadsweeper who went deaf. Booms! Lived in the council houses. Remember him? Invalided him home. No sooner off the trooper at Liverpool, his hearing comes back. Medics claimed it was a miracle. Never seen anything like it. Same thing happened to me at Neuf Chapelle. Next show of course."

"Oh is that where you became deaf? Where is Polly, Major?"

"Came round an angle in the trenches and ran into a Boche patrol. Their chaps hooked it and my chaps hooked it. Left high and dry. You'd suppose I'd caught leprosy. Jerry lobbed a grenade over his shoulder. Blew m'boot off."

"Where can I find Polly?" I yelled. "And why did it not blow your foot off as well as your boot?"

He had paused, plainly brooding over that long gone encounter in Flanders Fields.

"Left me for dead," he cried indignantly. "Hooked it! And called themselves Englishmen! Propped m'self up as best I could and watched m'other boot fill up with blood.

41

Wondered who would break it to m'poor old mother. Saw her plain as I see you, Hetty, sitting there in her kitchen. Clock ticking away on the mantelpiece between our pair of Staffordshire dogs. (My sister Georgina took them when she married – fancied 'em m'self.) Still as a church in her kitchen. My mother's not Georgina's. Still woman herself. Give me a still woman every time. . . ."

(Had he forgotten me? Dare I sidle off to seek Polly?)

"Next thing I know there was George Emmott, the adjutant, kicking back the patrol and cursing. Can't repeat his language to a well-brought up girl, Hetty. Put his boot up that corporal's backside. Last thing I remembered. That! Came-to in a field hospital. Poor old George! Didn't come back from a shifty next night. Caught in the wire they told me. Haled from some spot in Rutland. Ever been there, Hetty?"

Oh dear, I thought. Poor old George indeed! What if he's floating around hearing us remembering him? But he might quite like that.

"Worse than this show, Neuf Chapelle!" the Major shouted, shaking his hoary locks and prodding away at Majuba Hill once more. " 'Picnic this!' I told Booms. 'Picnic!' "

At this juncture in the history of British Battles, Mariana came in from the hall and I told her all that had befallen me.

"Oh the awful brute!" she cried. "Come upstairs and show me in case I'm called to give evidence. Down with your knickers."

"What does your bum look like normally?" she asked. "There's no livid weals as they say in the papers. Not that I won't swear that there were, if it comes to court. And what's a livid weal look like in case they cross-examine me? Oh, of course you must stay here now. Grandpa will love it; you know how well you two get on together and I must say there are times when I'd welcome a relieving force when he drags me off to Flanders Fields. 'They left me for dead,'" she shouted in a gruff voice. "'Hooked it! M'own chaps! And called themselves Englishmen!'" And this, unworthily, set us giggling.

And she was quite right: the Major did not seem to think it odd that I had moved in with them. The old do not seem to bother their heads with fiddling little details like the rest of us. It is enough for them to be alive I suppose.

Mr Birtwisle deals his last card

Of course I didn't believe for a moment that Birtwisle would give in. He well knew that, in Fenland, chilling reasons were thought up for anyone doing almost anything and so was not going to have it noised abroad that his Ethel had bolted. If I had just quietly disappeared on a train and before witnesses, it could have been put around that I was staying indefinitely with a distant aunt to recover from brain-fever brought on by A-levels. But being at The Grange was plain proof that I had fled for refuge.

On the evening when he turned up, we were in Mariana's bedroom. "It's not fair," she was complaining. "Me with a face full of freckles and built like a front-line forward and you long-legged and rangy, green eyes and, if that wasn't enough, that fab head of hair."

"Ginger," I said modestly.

"Flame-coloured," she said firmly. *"And* the way you can switch to good old Operation Enigma. Talk about Mona Lisa! Oh, I'd give anything to have your eyes: it's hopeless trying to make blue ones flash."

She turned to the wardrobe mirror and, to cheer herself after one or two eye-flashes that went off at half-cock, did a few compensatory hip rolls.

"Thank heaven humans can't see their own bums," she went on. "Just look at me. From behind who could mistake me for anything but a healthy child-bearer. Then, spin me around and what do you see. A face like an open book!"

There's always your boobs," I comforted her. "You said yourself that they are quite striking. If ever Galahad offers you a lift on his cross-bar do take great care not to turn quickly or you will strike him from the saddle."

"So long as he doesn't blunt his lance," she cried, recovering her good spirits. And we still were giggling when a banging began on the front door. The Morris Minor was parked in the drive.

"Don't hang back," Mariana cried. "You're quite safe with me. He won't dare to assault you before witnesses, But if he does try, you dive for his legs and I'll pin his arms. Then we'll sit on him." And she charged down to the hall and, after a time, reappeared with Birtwisle at her heels.

"Not a single inch further," she cried fiercely. "Not one inch! Stay just there and say what you've come for. Now my man – what do you want?"

How extraordinary! I thought. Before today I have never noticed how large Polly really is. Surely she has swollen?

"What do I want!" he barked. "What do I want? What do you think I want? I want her. Our Ethel. That's what I want."

So far the Major was quite oblivious to what was going on almost under his nose, his attention being fully absorbed by a more distant battle outside Ladysmith. And he only raised the siege and rallied to our battlefront when his grand-daughter shook him roughly and pointed histrionically at our visitor.

"He says he's come for Hetty," she yelled in his ear.

"For Ethel!" my ex-father snarled, butting his head towards me.

"He says he wants Hetty so he can beat her up again," she shouted.

"Eh?" the Major said, peering in his guest's direction, seeking to focus eyes and brain. Evidently he did not succeed because he heaved himself from the armchair and stumped forward to take stock of the situation.

Then he turned to Mariana. "Who is it, Polly dear?" he shouted. "What does the fellow want? Whatever he's collecting for, give him something and tell him not to come back. But mind – he's to have nothing if he's one of those Buddhists."

Her presence of mind was truly impressive.

"That time at Neuf Chapelle," she screamed back. "He's one of that lot. The ones who scarpered when the Boche blew your boot off. He's the corporal, the one George Emmott booted back."

"Oh, he is, is he!" the Major shouted. "Why weren't you shot, you coward?" He hobbled back, steadied himself at the mantelpiece and began fumbling up the wall for his cavalry sabre.

"You old madman!" Birtwisle cried, utterly confused by this talk of battles long ago but, nevertheless, prudently backing towards the open door. "You should be put away. I'll report you to the Council. And the Police. Threatening behaviour whilst harbouring a runaway."

"Eh?" the Major shouted, frustrated in his efforts to get at his weapon whilst keeping an eye on the foe.

"He says, given half a chance, he'd do it again," Mariana cried. "He says he wished you'd had time to bleed out your life into your other boot, the left one, as you've often told us."

Her Grandpa must have cottoned on because he renewed yet more furiously his effort to unhook the fearsome weapon, consequently bringing down a tea-caddy and an avalanche of spare change meant for the milkman and the weekly newspaper bill. But Birtwisle had fled. With one leg prudently inside the Morris, he shook a fist at us or (who knows?) at the malign gods in their heavens (lowering as usual).

"That's done it, Mariana," I said, quite heady with excitement. "But you may have overdone it."

"He's gone, hasn't he?" she replied smugly.

"Ah, but he will return. And not alone. His next visit will be with the police or the NSPCC or a solicitor's clerk in his train. You don't know him; he is a simmerer. Give Birtwisle twenty-four hours and he will be at the boil again. So tomorrow morning I shall buzz off. It really has been wonderful of you to shelter me but I want . . ." and dried up.

"Want what?" she demanded.

"Well — want to do this and that," I replied lamely. "I shall tell you when I've done it. There will be a very long letter, Mariana."

The Major interrupted us: he was running the ball of a thumb along his sabre's edge.

"He's hooked it, Grandpa," Mariana yelled. "Like he did at Neuf Chapelle."

"Ah," he muttered darkly, "And this time there'll be no George Emmott to boot him back. Poor old George! I'm a churchman, but there are times when I have m'doubts. Simply not good enough to snuff out chaps like Old George. But sometimes I have the fancy that he's still around and looking in on old comrades."

"Oh dear!" Mariana sighed, "I simply can't bear the idea of growing old, Hetty: sometimes he says things that make me want to blub."

Jordans Bank, Farewell!

There was our late summer smell of smoking stubble in the air as, next morning, we set off across the fens on the mile hike to Sinderby le Marsh Halt.

"Present my felicitations to Miss Braceburn," I reminded her. "And, for goodness sake, do not paint too hysterically dark a picture of my plight: you really must take a grip on your flights of fancy, Mariana. Just tell her that I am taking off like that chap we did in the IVth Form. Remember him? Josef Conrad's *Secret Sharer*. You know – the one who swam for it that tropic night. 'A free soul, a proud swimmer striking out for a new destiny. . . .' – I am pretty sure those were the words: Conrad usually says everything twice. Remember *The Secret Sharer?* Well, never mind. Miss B will."

"She'll be a bit pooped. She may suppose that she's somewhat to blame for your mess. Her dawg. . . ."

I considered this.

"No, I think not. Although Mustafa may have been a catalyst – yes, that certainly is a possibility. And tell her that my last words were that I shall watch my colons. She can give that whatever meaning she chooses."

We strode sturdily on through the beet fields.

"And am I not to tell her what you said about having done with Eng. Lit.? And about life not turning out like Bob Browning said it would? Don't deny it. That's what you said."

"Did I say that?" I exclaimed unbelievingly. "No, you are not to tell her. My wrestling match with Birtwisle must have thrown me off mental balance too."

"You did. I recall exactly what you said – 'Beautiful Evelyn

47

Hope is dead — So what?"

I considered this. "I may give him another chance," I said.

A lorry heaped with grain ground past us; the EEC mountain was going to be more insurmountable than ever this year.

"It's going to be a sensation when I break it to the Sixth Form. Can you imagine Ronnie's face?"

"Then you must console him," I said. "There still are a couple of days of term left. Manoeuvre him into my vacant seat beside you on the bus. I have read that touching people is more eloquent than words. And there are your boobs; it behoves us to employ profitably whatsoever gifts God hath given us. Take the window seat and make a point of turning lingeringly to discuss features of the passing scene."

We burst into loud laughter and as, far off, the Wisbech pay-train rose above the horizon, we linked arms and sang — Polly's nasal contralto, with me striking a rather interesting reedy note —

> Tous les jeunes filles et garcons amoureuses,
> Les yeux dans les yeux et les mains dans les mains . . .

"Oh do look back," she broke off. "I'm sure that's Ronnie pedalling like mad after us. However did he find out: I didn't let on."

"You will be able to hitch a lift home," I said. "On his cross-bar. Fancy! His knees pumping all around you and his hot breath on your neck."

"N'est il pas amoureux?" she moaned. "All the same I wish I was coming with you, Hett. And but for Grandpa I would. Oh I know all sorts of absolutely exciting things are bound to happen to you. Here, take this; it's all I could raise." And she fumbled a few coins into my pocket. "Hey, where are you going? It's this platform for London."

"I have had a change of heart," I cried as I ran. "My goal is

Birmingham." Then I kissed her affectionately and climbed aboard.

"You do mean to come back to Jordans Bank, don't you?" she asked plaintively.

"Not in this life," I replied (for my blood was up).

She looked so cast down at this stout affirmation that I hurriedly promised that, when the time was ripe, I would send my address and arrange for the Major and herself to visit wherever I had come to rest. This cheered her up no end and I completed a rehabilitation into her usually cheerful self by reporting that, whilst looking up at me, I distinctly had seen one eye flash twice.

The train already was on the move before Ronnie could dump his bike and dash onto the platform. "Hetty!" he cried. "Hetty, where are you going?" I gave him no more than a scornful glare but, although Polly was gazing adoringly at him, he looked so dejected that I relented and gave the poor fellow a perfunctory dismissive wave. Then I pulled up the sash, found a seat and looked my last on the fields, dykes and embankments and on distant Jordans Bank.

Oh dear! I thought, this is my childhood slipping away, and I sank deeper into despair, wondering for how long people would remember me. Would Ronnie? Would Miss Braceburn? But Ronnie would have freshly laundered and ironed choir-girls falling thick as autumn leaves at his feet whilst organs moaned and stained-glass sunbeams twinkled in his hair. And at Waterland High there always would be a succession of promising pupils to gaze idolatrously at Miss Braceburn. Surely someone besides Polly and the cat, Percy, would mourn my passing? But who? Alas!

Then we reached Peterborough.

A rest on life's way

I had an hour and a half's wait and took myself off to the abbey church which always calms me: why I am never sure. Perhaps just because it is there and has been for a thousand years — a shaped stone quarry turned turtle. Once under ground. Now upon it. So I sat alone by the west door and dived, drowning in its immensity. And stillness. And emptiness. So that, when I surfaced at the railway station, waiting for the train on its way from Norwich, I felt buoyant and quite myself again, ready, aye ready to outface fate, come what may.

An Extraordinary Encounter

And, of course, almost at once things took a sharp turn for the better. For only a few miles westward along the line I espied a taxi bashing along making for Melton Mowbray Station and with less than even odds that whoever was in it would catch the train. Then it was lost from sight behind malt kilns . . . then wagon repair-sheds . . . platform palings . . . ticket office. We stopped (wontedly), paused; no one got off, no one got on. And no birds sang.

A short pinkish man with a truly splendid moustache dashed like mad beneath the arch, brushed aside a gawping porter, sprinted neck and neck with the train, tore open my door, flung in his elegant hat, then a suitcase, then an umbrella, then himself. "Well done, sir!" I cried. "Well run! Oh jollywell run!" (In mis-spent pre-Braceburn days I had been a devotee of the works of Angela Brazil picked up at jumble sales.)

He lay back panting but acknowledged my congratulations with a slight bow.

"You caught it," I reassured him. "Providing, of course, that this is the train you had a mind to catch. We are on our way to Birmingham. Are you travelling far?"

"Yes," he gasped. "Australia!"

Australia! To Australia! How absolutely exciting life is, I thought, as Ayers Rock, Alice Springs, Bradman the Batsman and Kangaroos sprang to mind.

But then he started and turned pale. Heavens, what now! I wondered, fearing that my Girl Guide First Aid might not be up to coping with a heart attack. He snatched a splendid blue silk handkerchief from his breast pocket, carefully arranged it behind his round head and leaned once more against the upholstery, still pale but calm again. I watched absolutely fascinated until Miss B's stricture came to mind. Then I watched fascinated.

"Young woman, I had a friend once," he began solemnly in cultivated tones. "A very dear friend, Gerald Merryweather (who was with me at Dartmouth). And he caught a most dreadful disease from leaning his head against a First Class compartment's upholstery between Crewe and Stoke-on-Trent. This contagion spread first over his scalp and then his face. During what was left of his brief and ruined life, on entering a restaurant, he draped a towel over his head and remained beneath it whilst eating the meal."

No one before had troubled to draw my attention to this likelihood and, feeling rapport was called for, I followed suit with an inferior and shamefully unclean handkerchief.

Nodding approval, he then took me further into his confidence by telling me that another and more fortunate friend had discovered a goldmine in the Queensland out-back and had invited his help to exploit this bonanza. As he elaborated the hardships, the wild yet beautiful locale, the amiable qualities of his friend and a certain accumulation of great wealth, I felt half-inclined to ask if they had any need for a helpmeet to cook, wash and sew on buttons. But I was still mulling this over, perplexed by likelihood of insuperable expense should my A-levels justify a return from exile to England, when the train drew into the gloom of Birmingham's New Street Station and settled the matter.

"Ah!" he said, "Now I change here for Avonmouth. For the boat y'know. None of my business but I fancy you too are out on your own. Some small crisis? No, no, no, do not deny it; it is plain for all interested persons to see. Also that you are set on making a way for yourself? Yes? Am I right?"

So I told him that he was right.

"Well," he went on, "We all need a little help along life's weary way. Did m'self once upon a time. This is the best I can do. Have a long way to go y'see." And he fished out a wallet and pressed a couple of fivers into my hand.

"And here – take this silk handkerchief to remember me by; I like being remembered. Regrettably, a temperamental weakness. And such a handkerchief would be de trop in the bush."

He raised his hat and was gone.

Then, as I stood bewildered amongst the push and shove of a shopping concourse which had elbowed its way alongside the trains, he was back at my side once more.

"I suppose you have not had the misfortune to have visited this remarkable place before?" he said. "So where will you lay your head tonight? You are very young."

I told him that I didn't know.

"Ah!" he said, shaking his head, "I thought as much. This will never do."

Then, taking a used envelope and a pencil which (in touchingly antique style he licked), he painstakingly wrote an address. "Rose has a big heart," he said, "and has known hard times herself. It will be enough to say that I sent you, for her to find you a bed until you find your feet. Perhaps you will be kind enough to convey to her my continuing affection? You will? How kind of you. Thank you! Well, who knows, who knows – perhaps we may meet again."

Then he really *was* gone.

Rose Gilpin-Jones

The address given me was a terrace of enormous Victorian residences, their stucco and peeling paint mourning better times. At one end, the street's view was closed by a smoke-soiled church in the Baroque style and, at the other, by a derelict brass foundry.

Much may be learnt of a householder's domestic regime by the manner in which a front door is opened to visitors. And, at no. 27 there was no laborious drawing of bolts and rattling of chains. Instead, it was flung ajar with a flourish which must have thrown into speechless confusion innumerable double-glazing and cavity wall-filling persuaders. A large woman, bringing to mind a once lovely but now overblown begonia, looked down upon me.

"Yes, yes, I am Rose Gilpin-Jones," she said loudly but not over-bearingly. "But who are you? Speak up. No, more loudly than that. You have a good head of hair. It's high time and past that I took my once fair locks to a hairdresser. Oh, so Douglas sent you, did he? How very interesting! I was thinking of him only this morning whilst making the beds. You do look abject at the foot of my steps. This is not a white-slave agency. Do come in. Did he invite you to marry him?"

"I am afraid that he didn't offer his other name, his surname," I told her. "And no, neither did he offer marriage. But he did suggest that you might find me a room in your house – only for a day or two, of course."

I was unable to look her in the face whilst uttering this forlorn plea – although her next words implied that she may not have heard it, for she was examining (with the greatest attention) the crossed-out address on the used envelope which he had given me. "Good Lord!" she was murmuring, "This is his mother's hand-writing. So the old girl still lives!"

"Ah, so you know Douglas, my ex," she mused. "He's the Gilpin. Mr Jones came later. Douglas is an acquaintance of longstanding perhaps? May I keep this envelope? Is it too much to hope that he gave you the letter inside it?"

"Oh no, I have known him only for something less than

one hour. We met for the first time on the train; he was travelling to Australia. No, there was no letter. But this is his handkerchief. Perhaps you might care to have it?"

"Thank you," she said. "Thank you, yes I would," (and smelled it).

"Oh dear, what fond memories a man's scent brings to mind! Ah the times we had! So he's gone off to Australia this time, has he? The diggings, I suppose?" And took another long sniff at the handkerchief.

I replied that he had mentioned a small goldfield and the hope of immense riches. Unaccountably, this sent her off into screams of quite violent laughter. In fact, she rocked to and fro and began to gasp for more air. Not wishing to appear astonished, I turned away to examine a distinguished long-case clock ticking placidly away in a dark corner of the very spacious entrance hall. On its brass dial was engraved,

Ah, how doth beauty like a dial hand
Steal from his figure and no pace perceiv'd
Edmund Kirby
Daventry
1890.

Of course, it should have read 'yet' not 'how' — '*Ah, yet doth beauty . . .*' and I wondered who Edmund Kirby could have been to presume himself competent to edit Wm. Shakespeare and even, by implication, to have suggested that he had written the lines. Then I turned back towards Mrs Gilpin-Jones, now quite recovered.

She was a hefty creature, lavishly overflowing her bone-structure and had a large mouth with a full set of strong teeth which looked unusually eager to take a bite. There was not the slightest doubt that she would be more than a match, either in love or war, for the general run of oppressors (such as Mr Birtwisle) and that, if she was on your side, all fear could be cast aside.

We conducted the rest of this interview at the foot of a wide staircase alongside a green baize notice-board criss-crossed by elastic bands holding down exciting envelopes festooned with foreign stamps and cryptic messages – *To Await Arrival, Return to Sender after One Month*.

"If this is all your baggage, Hetty," she said, "You must have left home in haste."

I admitted this.

"You have a cultured tone of voice. Is your father a country parson?"

I told her No, but that in an endeavour to rid myself of a Fenland whine, I had modelled myself upon a Major Horbling and on Miss Braceburn, a teacher much admired by me. Then, because (despite her excessive merriment) I felt that Mrs Gilpin-Jones was a person who might be trusted, I added, "To tell you the truth, I am a runaway."

She received this news calmly.

"Ah well," she said cheerfully. "I've done some running away myself in my time. I fled from one boarding-school at thirteen and another at seventeen and have repented neither flight. My intention, on each occasion, was to light out for the goldfields of Colorado – (I was a fan of Bret Harte, an American who wrote books). But, the first time, I was trapped by my house-mistress at Malvern Links Railway Station and, on the second, by Douglas. We met by chance at Paddington. And, before I hardly knew what was afoot, I had become his child-bride."

This confession sent her off into another fit of laughter. Then she told me that she had an attic free at the moment and that I could have it until I found somewhere better.

"I suppose that you haven't a job?" she said.

I told her that I felt confident of finding one soon, having good O-levels and being ready and willing to take on almost anything. However, until then, I could not afford to pay much rent but hoped that she would trust me. "I am afraid that I am down to nineteen pounds plus the ten which Mr Gilpin insisted that I must take."

"So he forked out a tenner," she said, quite dewy-eyed, "Well, he always was a softie, poor fellow. He must have taken to you, Hetty. He always had a thing about tall red-heads. I once had my own dyed for a few weeks just to titillate him. Are you quite sure that he didn't invite you to be his child-bride?"

She once more burst into only half-suppressed laughter. "I expect you brought me to mind – also on the run and alone on a railway station. Now please – no nonsense about the rent. You don't look a big eater and, anyway, you can work your passage about the house – tidying things, washing up, burning the toast, straightening beds, carrying trays to those too broken down to leave their rooms. Then, when we know each other better, I'll decide what sort of job to help you find: this may not be easy because I can see that you are an intellectual."

I admitted that I supposed that this was true and this, once more, sent her off into mad laughter. "As a matter of fact, I've been feeling a bit low these last few days," she gasped. "It must have been God manifesting himself here below in the unlikely form of Douglas who sent you to my door. And you talk like a book: I can scarcely wait to hear your tale of woe. But now you must be looking forward to a wash, a lie-down on your bed and perhaps a dish of baked beans."

As we trekked to the second-floor she told me that she would be putting me next to a Mr Peplow. "He is all alone in the world (I collect them) and says he's a retired bank-manager. He's never mentioned a wife. Looks a hidebound old bachelor, poor fellow.

"He can't sleep at night because of his legs. Shrapnel from the War he says. Oh and he keeps himself quite clean and he's too shaky on his pins to bother you. Now you know as much about him as I do, Hetty. And what did you say your second name was?"

Number Twenty-Seven

Although I had left Jordans Bank and the Fenland no more than a few hours earlier, it already was a world away and, with Osokosie and the Birtwisles tidied away into the past's lumber-room and now lying upon my bed gazing contentedly at the skylight, I felt that the day had gone well with me. And I congratulated myself on celebrating this propitious beginning by changing my name to Miss Beauchamp — and that, at a moment's notice.

And now, how exhilarating it was to be here, in a great city! This was no time to be abed.

So I climbed upon a chair and pushed up the skylight's pane. Far off, to the south, was to be seen what I learnt later was the Observatory, nearer, the dome of Cardinal Newman's Oratory and, yet closer, the H.P. Sauce Works and Aston Villa. Yes, that is how I saw Birmingham on that July afternoon. And that was almost all I ever saw. From then on, most of my time was spent inside No. 27 for when, after the final washing-up, I emerged, day had become night and I might as well have been Anywhere.

On the boarding-house's second floor, there were four of us — Matthew, a very small, very black man from Sierra Leone, who was Curate at St Barnabas's; a woman seen once and then only on the day we both left and of whom Mrs Gilpin-Jones knew nothing except that, for some reason or another, she had bicycled across Turkestan dressed as a boy. And behind my party wall, there was Mr Peplow, the retired banker with shrapnel in his legs. For some days I only *heard* him but this was enough for me to know that, when we met, we should get on very well together.

In the early night-time, it was like old times at Waterland High, times when I still rejoiced in Eng. Lit., to hear him mumbling verses (to relieve the pains in his legs), verses which he had committed to memory as a schoolboy. It was his custom to open with that sombre military episode memorialising *The Burial of Sir John Moore at Corunna* and, that done, to continue with the lesser known *Lament for Thyrsis* (which we had done in the Fifth Form),

> Too quick despairer, wherefore wilt thou go?
> Soon will the high Midsummer pomps come on,
> Soon will the musk carnations burst and swell. . . .

And drowsily listening behind our wall, I was convinced that the old gentleman, lying there in the darkness (and for once forgetting his legs) was harking back to a country boyhood, was breathing country smells, recalling country sounds. And, indeed, when I came to know him better, he confirmed that this was so and, also, that he was not a bachelor (as Mrs G-J had supposed).

"Matthew Arnold, a very much under-estimated chap, Miss Beauchamp!" he told me. "Hilda, my dear wife, thought most highly of him. Oh yes, indeed she did. 'He is a summer poet,' she often said. 'He has written of winter in the hills but his heart was never in it. Summer was his season, summer by the stripling Thames' (You will recall the relevant lines, Miss Beauchamp?) And so, lying in the dark, I like to believe that it still is that same summer, when Hilda and I were young and first in love. So Thyrsis brings her back to me . . . if you follow?" And I told him that I did.

I never managed to hear out Thyrsis which is quite a lengthy affair and goes off into moralising towards its end. But it has its moments,

> Roses that down the alleys shine afar . . .
> And the full moon and the white evening star.

Poor Arnold, despite having to earn his bread as a school-inspector, had a very fine line in rural languor and those marvellous lines usually were the last which I heard before leaving Mr P to wander off down and along the dark riverside to meet his Hilda.

Miss Emma Foxberrow (1)

Well, now, as I already have said, each day lasted much longer than at Jordans Bank. Mrs Gilpin-Jones did not spare me. I only went off duty when we had cleared up for the four who ate at table, Miss Foxberrow who had her meals taken in on a tray and, finally, the two of us. (Mr Peplow did for himself on a gas-ring and how the Eastern Traveller managed I never knew.)

But I did not bewail my lot. After all, by a hairsbreadth I had escaped pinning to a telephone switchboard and there was ever a hope of a less inglorious future if A-levels went well. Meanwhile Brum was good enough and I quickly recognized that the hobnobbing with Mrs G-J was hastening on the growing-up process no end.

On two or three evenings each week I sped away and by supreme effort frequently presented myself at the Rep for the second half of a play or at the interval in a Town Hall orchestral concert (happily often when the box office had gone off duty). So usually I returned well after ten o'clock.

There, in its corner, the venerable longcase ticked comfortably on and, behind her door, the similarly venerable Miss Foxberrow babbled on too. Like Prospero's Isle, no. 27 abounded in strange sounds and airs that gave delight and hurt not.

"Oh do not be alarmed," Mrs G-J warned me. "Old Emma Foxberrow is well and truly round the bend and I ought to ask her to make other arrangements. But it was Douglas who begged me to take her in. (She was with his mother at Girton or so he said. Not that I believed him.)" Then, after plunging her nose into Douglas's handkerchief, she added, "And I feel that, if I insisted on her making other arrangements I should be letting him down. (But I ask you – Cambridge! Her!) Besides, the poor old wreck claims she has no kindred, anyway none with addresses in This World. Douglas's mother (Lady Gilpin, that is) was an intellectual like you, Hetty: I never cared for her," adding after jaundiced reflection, "Nor she for me. Would you say I was a light-minded woman, Hetty?"

No one, not even Mariana, had such a gift for irrelevancy as Mrs Gilpin-Jones.

"She goes maundering on half the night – no, not Lady Gilpin – Miss Foxberrow. (Mind you, she is actually not a 'Miss' at all. She's 'Mrs.') You should stand by her door and have a listen. Oh it's O.K. she won't know: she's hard of hearing and anyway she'd never catch you at it, she would trip over things. She's reliving her life. On and on. Or rather, back and back. All those she mentions . . . well, let's forget them. There was a time when I used to try to fit all the pieces together. But none of it made sense and certainly none of it fitted in with what Douglas told me when he dumped her on me. (Not that anything he said was much to go by: that was part of his charm.) All the same, the poor old thing must have been pretty enough once. Though she's shrunk, the bones are there. You have good bones too, Hetty."

I considered that it was simply splendid that, when he was not following fate and fortune to the Antipodes, Douglas was such an influence for good. Despite his domestic short-comings, it seemed that he always must have been on the look-out for wayfarers in distress and forwarding them on to Mrs Gilpin-Jones.

So, when next night I came in, I paused at Miss Foxberrow's door and, as Mariana would have put it, plugged in.

"Oh George," she was saying, "I should have taken you when you asked me. Oh, don't hold it against me for ever. Please! Oh, why was I so wilful? It was Cambridge did for me. All head, no heart!" And she began to sob bitterly.

"Miss Foxberrow insists that she is a Cambridge graduate," I told Mrs. G-J next day as I washed the breakfast crocks whilst she was slicing runner beans.

"Cambridge!" she cried scornfully. "The nearest she may have come to Cambridge was seeing the Boat Race – that is if he ever let her out of that house by the river in Putney. My! He was a wrong 'un! Oh what a brute George Harpole was! Douglas said he knew it the minute he clapped eyes on him. (That was when he went with Lady Gilpin to their wedding.) He led her a fair old dance. Kept a string of women on the fortune her father left her. (He was in Boots and Shoes.) And, when the last penny was down the drain, he beat her. (Hetty, do be very, very careful whom you marry: batterers abound in Britain.) But she took it without uttering a cry. (One learns that in boarding schools.)"

"And then? What happened then?" I asked.

"Oh, he kept it up. Without pity. Pity! There was no pity in him. Oh the devil! But her cries were heard in heaven."

"Earlier you said that she did not cry," I managed to squeeze in.

"Her silent cries! God is never around when he's wanted, but for once he tuned in and handed Harpole his come-uppance. No, for a change, he didn't let yet another scoundrel get away with it. In a sodden rage Harpole killed one of his women, the one he kept in West Bromwich. Cut her throat from ear to ear."

"What with?" I asked.

"A sword-razor. My father had one; never used a safety in his life. (Well, that's not true; he used one on his deathbed. Couldn't stand up then you see. The sound of stropping is part of my childhood.) Douglas told me it was a shocking sight. Blood slopped all over the shop and the woman had only paid for the furniture to be covered the week before. They wouldn't have caught him but for it dripping through the bottom flat's ceiling as they were eating a late Sunday breakfast."

"Like Tess of the d'Urbervilles," I said.

"Who? Oh her! I didn't see that happening in the movie," she said crossly.

"Then they must have censored it," I said. "Miss Braceburn once told us that film-goers have not so strong stomachs as novel-readers."

"She went regularly every Sunday afternoon to see him in his condemned cell," Mrs G-J went on. "But even in there, he had to be restrained from having a bash. On the day they hung him, naturally they wouldn't let her in to forgive him and it was the wettest day for years. The floods were out. Then, when the clock struck twelve, they topped him."

" 'Strapped, noosed, nighing his hour/He stood and counted them and cursed his luck/And then the clock collected in the tower/Its strength – and struck,' " I murmured absent-mindedly (lapsing from my resolution to be done with the poets and their unworldly ways.)

"Good gracious – we've got through that heap of beans

and scarcely noticed it," said Mrs G-J. "What were you saying, dear? Who struck who?"

Miss Foxberrow (2)

It was quite bewildering – this garbled account of Miss Foxberrow's biography. Could it possibly be that both had confused the identity of the man or men in her life? Yet surely the poor old lady might have been expected to remember whether or not she was a Mrs or a Miss! And which of us is likely to forget whether or not a husband has been hanged? but when next I paused at her door, she still was at this same stage of disturbed recollection. "Oh George etc. . . ." she was calling distressfully.

Whatever did she read at Cambridge? I wondered. Not philosophy or she would have known better than to marry a batterer. So it must have been Eng. Lit. which she then took so seriously that it went to her head. (This, as I now knew, could easily befall the unwary.)

I discussed this supposition with Mrs Gilpin-Jones but, as I might have known, she would have none of it. "Oh nonsense! Utter and ridiculous nonsense! Harpole was just a plain unvarnished brute. Nothing more, nothing less," she cried passionately. "Douglas told me that, once, Harpole took the poor silly creature by the throat and squeezed till her eyes bulged. And she told Douglas that she recalled wondering what would happen if they popped out or if they were attached with gristle to their sockets."

(What an extraordinary sight that would have been, I thought. Him – the brute – without any warning getting one or both eyeballs splashed in his face.)

" 'Why she didn't kick him in the crutch as any decent

woman would have done, beats me. (Mind you do, Hetty, and no half-measures, if ever a man makes a grab at you. They're more sensitive there than us and it snuffs the sexual appetite quite dramatically.) And Douglas asked her just that.

"'Oh I doted on him too much,' the stupid creature said. 'And, anyway, in the end he left off, although I had blue finger marks there for days and had to wear a scarf.'

"Well, now that you know the truth about Miss Foxberrow, let's hear no more of your silly ideas. Real life is not like you intellectuals think it is."

Then she told me that she had a friend in the Education Offices who could find me a supply-teacher job when the new term began. "But you can still drudge here in the evenings," she added. "In lieu of rent, of course. Then, with your salary, you'll be able to afford a change of garb at Marks & Sparks: you can't keep wearing that gym slip or people will begin to talk. Never mind why; you'll understand some day and, if you don't, read *The News of the World*.

Miss Foxberrow (3)

Well, what may have been the truth for Mrs Gilpin-Jones by no manner of means satisfied me and Miss Emma Foxberrow still remained a fascinating enigma. So, a few nights later, I tried once more. It was quite rewarding for the action had moved away from Putney and on to happier times and climes.

"Do you remember Sinji, George?" she was crooning. "The lagoon and those palm trees and the trade winds blowing? And what was that song you used to sing at smoking-concerts when we were in Tampling St Nicholas? The song those horrid beery old Buffaloes used to bawl for? Wasn't that about trade winds? Wasn't it? Oh George, what a silly little fool I was. All head, no heart!

"I was so happy out there in Africa but, then, I didn't understand that it was only because you were there. I didn't, I didn't. And when I did, it was too late. Too late, too late! But you said that you'd never forget me. 'Never,' you said. 'Never!' And you promised that if ever I needed you, you would come. Oh George, do come and take me away. . . ."

If I had not known what a brute he was, I should have felt sorry for her. And even for him. For how could he come now that he was hung and in quicklime?

How awful love is! I reflected. Someone half-strangles you each second day and you have to keep on loving him. It was crazy. But it was thrilling. How I ached to tell Mariana: it was quite as dramatic as her mother's deathbed, poor creature.

Ivan the Terrible

As I have said earlier, no. 27's residents were a mixed lot. Besides Mr 'Not a drum was heard' Peplow and Matthew (sponsored and supported by the African Society for the Propogation of the Gospel amongst the English) and the woman who unaccountably had bicycled across Turkestan dressed as a schoolboy, there were a couple of elderly sisters who did nothing in particular but pray several times daily at St Barnabas's. These two had the more expensive rooms on the First Floor along with Ted who was a management apprentice at a brass tubes works (which paid his rent) and there was Ivan down there too. He was a Russian over here on a cultural exchange scheme funded by the British Council.

Ivan did not look in the least like the glum Russians shown

on TV, normally having medals pinned on their chests for churning out more nuts and bolts (and medals?) than anyone else. Astonishingly quickly he had picked up our western cult symbols and was dressed elegantly in M & S cords, a Warm & Wonderful pullover and a French leather blouson. And he was gay – in the old sense of that word, i.e. jocund, light-hearted – and not at all like the droopies in Chekov plays slodging around in carpet-slippers sighing about what they ought be be doing and not doing it. Ivan was very purposeful indeed and needed to be because, before he was recycled back into a tractor-driver on a collective farm, his raison d'etre was to put together a portfolio of photos illustrating Britain-as-it-is.

When I asked him why, he replied earnestly that Mr Kossov, his Kiev-control, had told him that Britons no longer were like books said they were. 'Take many picture. All time take picture' Mr Kossov say.

"My country not like books either," he said with a grin. "Bye bye Cherry Orchard. Bye bye Anna Karenina."

There was an uncomfortable pause whilst I assembled what little I knew of the USSR and we stared dumbly at each other. Then he said, "Mr Kossov say to find what people believe happening and then tell them that is what *is* happening. Why you laugh, Miss Beauchamp?"

And for the life of me I could not think why. Perhaps it was his believing face, a rare sight in Britain-as-it-is.

"Mr Kossov say foreigner remember Stalin and forget Stalingrad," he added. Well, what can one say to that? Nothing. It is true.

"I go to your football game on Saturday," he said. "With camera."

I shuddered.

"Sometimes I long for native land," he went on plaintively.

"That is understandable," I consoled him. "But do not

repine. Try Radio 3; you can take a healing bath of Tchaikovski almost any evening. But I am afraid that we shall have no snow for some weeks."

"Oh have found second home," he replied, cheering up. "I go sit in halls of your Nationalised Industries. Just like home."

"Good gracious – don't they throw you out?"

"No, no. Only men who smell. Not complain, not ask help – can sit for many hours. Like old times. Much happy memory. Watch faces of citizens who not get what they wait for. Faces of them wait long time in wrong line. Have photos. Mr Kossov say very good."

He warmed to his theme. "One show two girl talk ever so jolly at counter. Wait till line reach back to door, then put sign *THIS POSITION NOW CLOSED*. Have photo."

"Well," I said indignantly, "At least we do not have Siberia."

"Siberia, American propaganda," he said. "No Siberia in my country, Miss Beauchamp."

So much for Ivan.

And as for Ted, the tube-worker, his appearance was respectable and his demeanour modest. But he was distressingly illiterate.

('You're looking magic today, Miss Beauchamp' – as I served him rice pudding. But that was magic also – the pudding I mean.)

My favourite Resident

By far my favourite resident was my near neighbour, Mr Peplow, Mr Edward Peplow. When, eventually, we met I found that he was a tall old gentleman but now somewhat bowed and needing a stick. Although he tottered and much of his hair had gone, he seemed continually calm in mind and this fascinated me. It was as though he had schooled himself upon tenets recommended in Rudyard Kipling's adjurative poem 'If' and actually *did* treat triumph and disaster just the same. For his bearing and conversation announced that he was confident that nothing worse was likely to happen than what already *had* happened. He was altogether a quite admirable person, his only drawback being a disconcerting truthfulness whilst maintaining a steady gaze upon one's face.

Now and then I joined him for tea. This was no great burden to him for the menu never varied. First he made a strong brew of Brooke Bond and Lapsang ('To add a little je ne sais quois, Miss Beauchamp') and then spread before us a packet of Bath Olivers, one bone-handled knife and a small round box of Gentleman's Relish. A well preserved caraway seed-cake lurked in its deep tin and was given an airing but this evidently was no more than a gesture towards a festive look – for I was never offered a slice.

Conversation was desultory; neither of us saw TV, nor were we as concerned as we should have been about the awful state the world was in. It was on these occasions that I felt regretful that, because of my delayed discovery of life-as-it-really-is, I had forsaken the muses. For my host harboured a strong liking, verging on veneration, for our native bards and I should like to have echoed this enthusiasm (as, of course, once I would). And this I told him.

"Oh, never fear, try as you may, Miss Beauchamp," he assured me, "it will return. The springs of joy cannot be sealed. Oh yes, it will return and be a consolation and a comfort to you. As it is to me – as I wait here."

Good gracious, I thought. Here is yet another waiting.

"Waiting, Mr Peplow?" I asked politely, "Waiting for what?"

"Waiting for a touch on my shoulder to remind me that it is time to go," he replied calmly. "To quote my dear wife's father's favourite hymn –

Amen so let it be – absent from Him I roam
Yet nightly pitch my moving tent a day's march nearer home.

"And I am ready – gear packed and in good order. I am aged eighty-four, so well up in the queue and may as well wait here as anywhere.

"And it better not be much longer," he added reflectively. "My trousers have almost gone at the knees."

" 'This is best West of England tweed,' Hilda told me, 'and will just about see you out, Edward.' And, by jove, she was right (as she always was). And that was fifteen years ago come October."

He rubbed his knees.

"Almost down to a cobweb," he said complacently, his blue eyes glinting. "The last train had better be on time."

"You must not talk like that," I scolded. "You have years and years left yet."

He looked me steadily in the eye. "I sincerely hope not, Miss Beauchamp, and from now on, I shall call you 'Hetty'."

This was quite distressing. And, noticing this, he added disarmingly, "But I wasn't ready those nights over the Channel. That August in '44, none of us were. But I am now."

He told me this with a quiet satisfaction and there seemed little left to say. Not so.

"Up there, the sky full of tracer (or so it seemed), poor young Dexter dying in my arms, the kite lit up like a Christmas tree. Maybe seeing further along the coast a mate's Albacore, falling like a torch. I wasn't ready then. At times like that you wondered 'Is this it? Is this the finish? Oh please God, Not tonight.' "

He had continued to look steadily at me.

"It's a long time ago, Hetty. But sometimes now in the dark I am back there. And so are they. And then I wonder if it all has been a dream — if you follow me. A dream! Us I mean. And them. My wife, my mother. Brightwell, Bellenger, Ruskin . . . a dream. . . . Is it possible, do you suppose, Hetty?"

I answered that I was unaccustomed to such speculation and that answers to such questions ought not be shot off the cuff.

He agreed.

"But it would be comforting if if was so, don't you think?" he murmured. "I mean that we always had been and would always be and that, round some corner, we should find everything as once it was. And that poor old Mullett who bought it at Knocke-le-Zout and Bellenger and Ruskin (whose turns came later) would be there as once they were. And with us in that dream. . . ."

He laughed softly and leaned back.

"What about you, Hetty? What are you doing here?"

I was unsure if he meant what was I doing at no. 27 or what was I doing just being alive. Such questions are disconcerting: even extra tuition from Miss Braceburn had not prepared me for such speculation.

"I am waiting too, I suppose, Mr Peplow," I told him.

"Ah!" he said. "And for what, I wonder?"

We plainly had reached a non sequitur. So I asked, "Do you remember your mother quite well?"

"Better than I remember last evening's supper, Hetty," he replied. "And if I knew for certain that I was going to see her again, I shouldn't wait longer than tonight to take an overdose."

I determined not to be drawn down that distressing path again.

"What is it that you remember best?" I enquired.

"Why, her smile, of course!" he said.

"Oh, surely, more than that? That is not much to remember."

"It is everything, Hetty," he said firmly. "It was love. Will you not take another Bath Oliver?"

Oh dear, I thought, We must not go down that path either. And I replied, "No, thank you; we shall have supper about eight. What about your dear wife? You must recall her much more clearly."

"She had an amiable smile too," he said. "An exceedingly amiable smile – but then, she was an amiable woman."

"Well then?" I pressed him.

"But not like my mother's," (and laughed). "No one's smile is like one's mother's, Hetty. Surely you must know that. Any more than anyone can bake a cake like her. In my mother's case – a seed-cake. Yes, particularly her caraway seed-cake. I always supposed that she had learnt it from *her* mother."

He said this with such finality that I knew now was the moment to leave. As I turned at the door, he was smiling still.

But not at me.

I never asked him why he recited verse. But I guessed that when you are old, all the creaks and aches you ever had come back to remind you that you are and always have been no more than a bag of bones. And so Mr Peplow worked his way through all the lines he ever had learnt just to keep his mind off his legs until, unknowingly, he slipped into sleep.

And that night, after burying Sir John on the Field of Corunna (as was his wont), he began *A Lament for Thyrsis* and, when he reached,

> And round me too, the night
> In ever-nearing circles weaves her shade.
> I feel her fingers light
> Laid pausefully upon life's train
> And hope, once crush'd, less quick to spring again. . . .

I had an inkling of what we had been talking about and

decided that, if he ever raised the matter again, I would not reassure him about his likely longevity.

Reg Jones's Resurrection

I wish that I could report livelier happenings than inconclusive conversation with an old man and the overheard confusions of a feckless old lady. But, except for an occasional couple of hours in the evening, I was housebound and, although eager for something to happen to *me,* was quite ignorant of what might have been happening elsewhere. We were an enclosed society relying upon Matthew the curate, Ted and Ivan, to bring us glimpses of more stirring stuff. And things became worse when Mrs Gilpin-Jones sank into doldrums, her shouts of jolly laughter no longer stirring an echoing chime from tea-cups hanging hooked to the Welsh dresser.

It was not a happy time.

One evening, after supper, when I was grinding the stewingbeef which was to provide the protein in tomorrow's shepherd's pie, she plonked down on a kitchen chair and put her head in her hands.

"I can't stand any more," she wailed. "If this goes on, I shall sell up and follow Douglas to the goldfields whether he wants me there or not."

I waited expectantly.

"It is Reg Jones," she moaned distractedly. "He is trying to come back. All last week and now again this week he hasn't stopped trying. I have had no peace from him since a fortnight last Sunday. When he tried it on last time (which was before you came) I went and had it explained by the Spiritualists. They told me he was just across the Threshold and wouldn't budge an inch further. They said he was going on about being unfulfilled. They also said he wanted to come back so he could make it up to me for little unkindnesses he had done me now and then. Not that he ever did: he was the very soul of kindness."

She paused dramatically.

"Now he's at it again. It's too bad of him."

"Are you not alarmed?" I asked. "Particularly by night?"

She considered this for some moments.

"No," she answered seriously. "It's true we had our ups and downs. Tell me, who hasn't! But Reg wouldn't hurt a fly and, anyway, he wasn't very big. I was thirty when Douglas and me parted and only a year or two older when I took on Reg and he was well over the hill even then. Most of his hair and teeth had gone or were loose but, as you can imagine, we were madly in love. Yes, it's quite quite true – we couldn't get enough love. Neither of us. It was bliss."

"Didn't your parents offer any objection?" I asked. "After all, it must have seemed to them as if you were marrying an uncle."

"Well, I have to admit that, at first, they weren't too sold on the idea, particularly as he wasn't out of the top drawer (my first mother-in-law, as you know, being Lady Gilpin). But as I was their only chick, I suppose they decided to make the best of things, particularly as he had this house here in Brumbrum as well as some very good investments in the Gold Coast Company. But Daddy, in a roundabout way, did hint that Reg was too small for me."

"And was he?" I asked with interest (being tall myself).

"I never thought so," she said stoutly. "Mind you, then, I didn't spill over as I may do nowadays. Anyhow I'm convinced that short-legged chaps make the best lovers. Take Napoleon and Julius Caesar: I read in the paper that they were inexhaustible. Not that I was influenced by that: till the day he died, in a general way, I worshipped the ground he trod. And he knew it."

"Then do you want him back?" I asked.

This so exercised her that I was able to return my attention to the meat-mincing machine. "Do I want him back? I miss him: I'll grant you that. Yes, I do miss him. Not you understand, corporeally. That means. . . ."

"I am not illiterate," I told her stiffly. "And anyway, how could he be here with you, now he's dead?"

"No, of course, you're absolutely right," she agreed. "Well what I mean is that he didn't go away immediately. When I returned from the Crem he was still here. Does that make any sort of sense to you?"

"No," I said.

"Well I mean that I continued not switching on TV programmes which he couldn't bear. Just as if he was still alive sitting in his armchair. Now do you see? He used to get so cross about my having *Coronation Street* on, even when he wasn't in the house."

"Then (and like a flash), it came to me that now I was on my own. I could take you now, this minute, to the exact spot I was standing on. It was at Aston Cross. I was just feeling like fish and chips but knew he'd forbid it. He liked me plump, you see, Hetty. Plump but not fat! So I was just going into a greengrocer's to buy a lettuce when it struck me that it didn't matter what Reg thought now. Even if he was still hanging about (but non-corporeal, of course) he couldn't go on at me. Even if he actually appeared – well, he could only glare and I needn't look at him. So I bought a double-portion to make my point and ate them with my fingers going home.

"After that, it was like being a girl again." And she waved her big breasts at our kitchen's prevailing disorder and laughed triumphantly.

"If the Prince of Wales had made me an offer that minute, I

76

wouldn't have taken him on. What I really mean is that I felt I was as I had been before Douglas made me his child-bride – when I had a bedroom all to myself and could snore or roll around or listen all night to Radio Two if I wanted to and not having a man messing me about if he felt like it and I didn't. You are rather young to talk to about this sort of thing, Hetty. But you do want to grow up, don't you, dear? And having no mother. . . ."

I admitted to this not unworthy aim and added that a man once known to me, a Mr Birtwisle, had been the same as Reg, particularly about books and that it once had guiltily crossed my mind that, if he was dead, then I could read whatever I fancied and leave it lying around.

"There you are!" she exclaimed triumphantly, "You see, you *do* understand even though you have no mother."

This too I acknowledged (whilst reminding myself of why I had come to Brum and that, before I left it, I meant to have one).

"But sometimes," Mrs G-J went on, "Sometimes, when I am entertaining a friend, I imagine I can hear the door-knob turn and I think, Oh dear, Reg is back. Whatever will he say finding me like this?"

"Why don't you ask the Curate about him?" I interrupted.

"Who said my friend was Matthew!" she cried indignantly.

"Perhaps he learnt how to exorcise people like Reg at his theological college," I suggested.

"The Church!" she said scornfully. "Ha! Tell me what they can do about anything!"

"If you are not a believer, why do you go to church most Sundays?" I asked.

"To look at Matthew, of course," she replied as though I was a complete idiot not to have known this. "In his costumes. I like the one he has to wear around Christmas. Red with gold trimming. If only he would put on a false beard, as I have asked him, it would make him look just like Santa Claus; the kiddies would love it. Oh, if I was twenty years younger! Now tell me the truth, Hetty — do you suppose I would make a Vicar's wife? If you say No, I shan't be offended."

"Well, I am sure that most parishes would be all the more lively having you," I hedged. "And from what I have read, they would look up to you in Sierra Leone; it is said that they laugh there much more than we do. But then — what about Reg?"

"Matthew could cast a spell on him," she declared seriously. "Then he'd have to stay wherever Matthew had put him."

"What was your mother like, Mrs Gilpin-Jones?" I asked, embarking on give-and-take irrelevancy.

"Was?" she exclaimed. "Is! And likely to be for many a long year. She is alive and kicking all-comers up in Bridlington. And, as for what's she's like, I suppose I have to admit I do owe her something: after a girlhood endured in her company, I feel I can face up to most disasters likely to befall me. I shall leave the rest to your not-inadequate imagination, dear."

There was a knocking at the front door.

"I expect that will be him," she said absent-mindedly. "Go and see, please. Oh and by the way, I feel much better after our little chat. Quite myself again, in fact. Thank you, Hetty."

It was only Matthew who had forgotten his latch-key: he asked if Mrs G-J was in the kitchen.

As he passed I said, "If I were you, I should take unarmed combat classes when the night-schools start up in the autumn. In case Reg calls."

"What?" he said. "Beg pardon, Miss Beauchamp? Reg? Whatever are you talking about? Whoever is Reg?"

A letter lay on the mat and it was from Miss Braceburn.

'You have done splendidly, my dear, and all at Waterland High are proud of you; poor Spendlow is beside himself. Top A's in Latin and in literature and another in sociology (which we can disregard because it is something you will grow out of). . . .'

I returned to the kitchen. "I have done rather well in my A-levels," I reported modestly.

"Oh!" Mrs G-J said abstractedly, "Oh, you have, have you. Did you say A-levels? Tell me about it some other time: I'm just popping upstairs to take Matthew, poor lamb, a cup of tea."

A Pursuit of Love

Next day, Mrs Gilpin-Jones was quite herself once more and, over a Saturday mid-morning coffee, said, "At your age, you should have a boy-friend, Hetty. Join the Youth Club at Barnabas's. Matthew tells me there are some quite nice lads."

Resisting a half-inclination to tell her what a let-down my last 'quite nice lad', Ronnie, had turned out to be, I thanked her and said that I was quite content.

"Well, if you won't, you won't," she persisted. "Nearer home, there's Ivan, I suppose – although I can't believe that you would want to live in a snow hut in Siberia and be a socialist. And there is Matthew – but you must agree that he's more my style (as a mature woman)." Plainly she needed reassurance, so I agreed that he indeed was, adding that she would fit very well into a vicarage, if they had vicarages in Africa.

Yes, you're right, dear," she said smugly. "And I would soon pick up flower-arranging. Actually I'm quite fond of flowers. I suppose they do have them out there?"

She paused to consider other runners in love's field. "So

that only leaves Ted. He doesn't talk about his folks so they can't be up to much. But he's not afraid of work, I'll say that for him. I know he's only in industry but nowadays you never can tell: Lord Nuffield once kept a puncture-repair shop.

"On Sunday mornings Ted is into the black-economy with a fellow who fits exhausts and retreads. When I reminded him of the Fourth Commandment he didn't turn a hair. 'My boss says cars is the new religion,' he had the cheek to tell me, 'And we are the high priests.' "

She pondered this, perhaps approving her fairness in presenting Ted's pros and cons, before adding, "Besides anybody can see he's a demoniac and *they* always get whatever they're after. Reg was a demoniac."

I was not sure into which pan of justice's scales she intended this sweeping generalization to fall and, the mating season ending inconclusively, we continued stringing beans in reflective silence.

Amongst the Pre-Raphaelites

Actually, Ted, his black hair plastered to his scalp, was hanging about in the hall when, after lunch, I set out for the Municipal Picture Gallery. "Oh," he said boldly, "I've never been inside one but, if they're your cup of tea, I bet they're magic, so I'll come with you." And he did, beginning quite promisingly by walking several times around Jacob Epstein's double life-sized *Lucifer* they keep in their entrance-hall to menace visiting vandals.

"Carrying excess baggage, isn't he?" he remarked, taking an admiringly last look at the Fallen Angel's immense genitals. "For flying of course."

We proceeded to the pride of the gallery, a room of Pre-Raphaelites, bought during a 19th Century flush of civic pride in their local boy, Edward Burne-Jones, a dull man who painted competently dull pictures. How exciting! I reflected, All these dashing young men set on changing the way of things. Oh their bright visions of what England had been and might be yet again! Oh the crimsons and purples and those rebellious greens!

"They're not my scene," Ted announced flatly, unpleasingly bringing me back to earth. "Why do the chaps look so dim? Them and their droopy girl-friends! Take this one (sneering at Ford Madox Brown's absolutely glorious and perceptive emigrant picture, *The Last of England*). They should have had the guts to stick it out here: none of them looks at all keen to leave. Are we supposed to feel sorry for the drips? And all this Old-Time stuff" (waving an arm in comprehensive dismissal of *Chaucer reading at the Court of Edward III, The Long Engagement* and a galaxy of gorgeous Dante Gabriel Rossettis). "That lovesick chap in the round parson's hat, the one leaning on that tree in the wood! Look at his girl. You can tell from her face she's crazy to get down into the bracken with him. Though God knows how he'd cope with all the clothes painted on her, let alone those you can't see."

"There are some artefacts attributed to Neanderthal Man upstairs in the Museum," I said coldly. "Perhaps you should wander off and see how you relate to them. You will find them quite magic."

"Sarky!" he said. "Is there a tea-room? I'll pay."

There was no tea-room, so we set off back across New Street towards the northside bus terminal and thus had to pass Brum's very presentable Cathedral. Despite discouragement he followed me inside.

"These windows are also by Edward Burne-Jones," I told him. "Of course he did not actually make them; he designed them. Observe the west end. Is it not like an all-consuming conflagration? Do you not find it splendid?"

"No," he replied brutishly. "Plain glass for me! Windows are for letting in light."

Great God, I thought, And this after a century of popular education! If ever he is hung, you will not find me kneeling in the mud at the jail gate like Miss Foxberrow. And I felt that drawing his attention to Thomas Baskerville's headstone and its outrageous tale would be yet more pearls set before a swine so hurried onwards. Then, wishing my afternoon not to have been utterly wasted, I told him that I should alight three stops early so that I could look in on Mr Williams's Bookshop and that he must complete the journey alone. "Today, Saturday, I believe you will find cream buns in your tea-time trough."

He grinned. "I'll come with you," he said. "Then later we can push our snouts in side by side. You're super-magic when you blow your top."

Mr Williams, although constitutionally on the frail side, had a true pioneer's spirit, bravely manning his civilizing bastion on the frontiers of the Inner City. He was ridiculously ill-equipped for life in the book trade, having actually read many of the books he was trying to sell and ever ready to discuss literature, even with those who used his premises for a free read. It was a paradox that here he was, hemmed in by dreary streets and a brutish populace, yet offering a decent bookshop; whilst Waterland, its rich peat oozing fat fortunes, supported no more than a multiple, stocking only sex and blood-soaked bestsellers.

I purchased *Silas Marner* (which I knew featured an abandoned baby) and was greatly encouraged when Mr Williams agreed with my supposition that George Eliot had become so boringly sick of writing *The Mill* that she dismissively drowned both hero and heroine in the Floss and a single paragraph. But it was impossible to develop serious conversation with my companion fretting at our elbows, his poor mind fixated with cream-buns.

Tidings from Jordans Bank

I had been almost one month in Brum before Mariana replied to my promised letter giving an address. The school year had ended, the Latin mistress had left to marry a widowed clergyman met on a tour of the Holy Land, the Caretaker's mother had run off with a rich gypsy, the Major was still retreating in good order across the Veldt and was now holed up in Mafeking, Ronnie had been offered a place to read divinity on the strength of his three E's and Miss Braceburn, (who had been told my whereabouts in strict confidence), had said that, in no circumstances was I to accept the place offered me by a teachers' college.

(Come on, Poll, I urged, you must know what I am waiting for. What about him?)

'Your late Dad still looks miffed,' she wrote. 'He doesn't look at me when we meet, but I know he knows I know where you are and would like to have a bash. And, as for the odious Sonny, he must be getting your share of the aggro; he creeps around like a whipped dog. How horrible it must have been having him for a brother. . . .'

She then showed unusual interest in Mrs Gilpin-Jones. ('Has Reg come back yet!'), Mr Peplow ('Keep me some fossil seed-cake'), Matthew and Ted the Magic Man. But it was poor old Miss Foxberrow who fascinated her. (Which was the truth – Mrs G-J's biography or Miss F's autobiography?) And, when she came for the promised weekend to no. 27, could she have a listen-in too?

'P.S. Ted sounds my type. I bet he goes for girls with big you-know-whats.'

Despite these juvenile effusions I was quite touched by her concern for my welfare. And when I asked if I could invite the Major and her for a short weekend, him having my room and her bedding down with me in the lounge, Mrs Gilpin-Jones readily agreed, adding that her father had been a Major or a Sergeant-Major or a Major-General (she could not recall which) and so had a leaning towards military men.

What happened in our Front Garden

The weather remained hot and dry, untainted yet by autumn's melancholy, and it was during these weeks that we had the race riot. Although it was shown time and time again on TV (which had been starved of watchable violence since the Miners' Strike and the Belgian football massacre), I was one of the very few who knew how it began.

Like that earlier affray between Mr Birtwisle and Miss Braceburn's Mustafa, I recall the circumstances precisely. It was Saturday and I was seated in the entrance hall by the longcase clock whilst awaiting the hour appointed for delivery of Miss Foxberrow's cocoa and butter-biscuits. I was reading *Silas Marner*, a novel whose rhythm well suited the steady tick-tock behind me. She, Miss F, was going on along the same lines as usual. ('Oh George, you promised. Yes you did, you did. You promised that just whenever your Aunt Susan died, we should have Quince Tree Cottage. . . .') But she was not providing any sort of competition to George Eliot in her more masterful mood.

There was a shot.

('Oh George, I should not have spoken those bitter words. Oh George, the many, many times I have regretted them' – whilst in the novel that other George's 'poor woman of low class' was perishing in the snow but with little Effie snuggled safely in her arms.)

It was a shot. Definitely!

Mrs G-J came from the downstairs toilet. "Didn't I hear a shot, Hetty? Yes, I'm sure I heard a shot. Didn't you think it was a shot?"

(Miss F was sobbing quite bitterly now and the other poor woman in the snow, about to expire from hypothermia, was optimistically commending Effie into God's hand.)

"The silly creature!" Mrs G-J said crossly. "We must dunk a valium tablet in her cocoa from now on. Oh, listen to her raving. She knows we're listening. Of course she does. That's why she's pretending they didn't hang him. Quince Tree Cottage! What a ho ho ho!"

There was another shot.

We both agreed on that.

So we gingerly opened the front door but things outside were going on much the same as usual – buses crawled by, people trudged past.

"It was a car back-firing," Mrs G-J pronounced. "Yes, that's what we heard. A car back-firing. Close the door, Hetty. Then make her cocoa and I'll start her off with half a pill to see if that's enough to shut her up so that the rest of us out here in the real world can have some peace."

Quite soon afterwards, when we had cleared up in the kitchen, I put out the milk-empties with Sunday's order and, to take the air, walked down to the front garden gate. And there, immediately before me and a half-stride out onto the road, a man was sprawled. It was quite extraordinary. Cars and buses were slowing down and steering gingerly past him, whilst citizens on foot cringed against our wall so as to keep a respectable distance from the poor fellow.

And there he lay in the gathering dusk.

So I went out, bent down and had a good look at him. He was a black man, a West Indian and there was a sticky mess around and upon him. So I hurried back into the house and told Mrs G-J.

"There you are!" she cried triumphantly. "What did I tell you: I knew it was somebody being shot. Of course, you don't remember the War so there's some excuse for you. A dead man outside our front gate, did you say? I expect he's from Fishfingerland. The cheek of it!" She put on an all-purpose burberry which Douglas long ago had retired, bustled out and crouched beside the corpse, first peering closely in its face and then pressing an ear to its chest. "He's dead all right," she said.

The poor fellow moaned.

"You see!" she exclaimed. "What nonsense! – he's not dead. Who said he was dead? But if he stays here he'll be squashed by a bus and then he will be. Pop in and tell Matthew to come and give him the last rites; he keeps them in that little black bag in his wardrobe. Just in case."

I reminded her that it was Saturday Evening Mass at St Barnabas's for those worshippers who couldn't get off during the week and who also worked Sundays. So we began to tug him towards safety.

"Heavens! What a weight he is," she grunted. Then, observing a couple of surviving skinheads dancing past, she shouted, "Hey you, give us a hand here."

Their answer was to turn up their radio to full blast and to trip gaily into the front garden where they heaved our huge ornamental terracotta urn from its pedestal to shatter upon the stone slabs beneath. "We haven't got one," one monster yelled. "Why should you?" They shrieked with laughter and danced off.

Buses and cars were still rolling past. Pedestrians glanced furtively at us and slipped by.

Then an old man on a bike came wavering down the road and, surprisingly, got off. "Oh dear!" he said, sounding worried and concerned, "Oh dear, dear! What have we here? Poor fellow!"

I told him that I believed that the man had been lying out in the road for quite a time.

"And yet no one stopped," he murmured. "Oh dear! Birmingham – I have lived here for most of my life. Whatever has become of us; we didn't used to be like this. Fifty years, even twenty years ago, half this street would have been out wanting to help. But now we all seem to be frightened of one another. Mind you, Madam," he panted, "I almost bicycled past myself and had to remind myself, 'You are a law-officer; you must not leave distressed citizens lying upon the public highway.' (I am Judge Lavery, by the way. I have been visiting the boys' club I started many years ago at St Barnabas's Mission Church.)"

When we had laid our burden upon the pavement, the old gentleman asked to be shown a telephone so that he could summon an ambulance and the police. But, no sooner were he and Mrs. Gilpin-Jones gone, than another black man appeared and demanded menacingly, "What goes on, man? Ya done him in, ha?" And, like magic, footpath and road were filled with his mates buzzing like angry bees.

"Them skinheads down the Trouter done him," someone screamed. It was enough. Once more I was alone with the poor fellow. It was all quite astonishing. Perhaps also to him for he groaned again.

Mrs G-J returned. "You'll never believe it," she announced. "There's another of them in our garden. I've only this minute spotted him, half-in and half-out of the shrubbery. And that one really *is* dead. So now we know what happened, don't

87

we! That chap shot this chap and then the first chap had the cheek to shoot himself in our front garden. I'll have to move houses once this gets into the *Evening Mail*.

I told her that I believed we had started a race riot.

"Then that's the last straw," she declared indignantly. "Now we shall be on TV as well. Run along to St Barnabas's and, no matter what he's doing, tell Matthew to get it stopped."

The Inner City Riot

And a riot it really was. Mercifully not down our street but down the next road and across a canal and so was over the border where the Inner City began. By the time I reached the smoking outskirts of battle, the windows of shops were bursting like small bombs, some percussioned by bricks and some by the heat of fires. And now, seeing people going in and out of windows instead of doors brought home to me what a sheltered life I had led in Jordans Bank.

It was fascinating to recognize which were the intelligent looters. First, these had raided a perambulator and push-chair shop so that, whereas their dimmer brothers could make off with only one item, these bright sparks loaded up a colour TV, a video to supplement viewing hours and cartons of beer to deaden their critical faculties.

Naturally I looked anxiously to discover how Mr Williams's bookshop was faring and, saw that, although his window had burst in the heat, no one was stealing his stock, even though he had erected an inviting display pile of current best-sellers. So much for the teaching of English Literature in our schools! I thought indignantly, Not a single volume looted!

Whilst I was still seething, an elderly lady, obviously a gentlewoman who had come down in the world, left St Barnabas's and, sheltering behind Matthew's Wayside Pulpit (WHERE WILL YOU BE ON THE DAY OF JUDGMENT? – under which some irreverent oaf had sprayed, 'Waiting for the 13A Bus') viewed with amazement the prospect before her. She then ventured to the top of the flight of steps and appeared to be weighing alternatives of a bed in a pew or her Sheltered Accommodation for the Elderly further along the battle lines.

Bravely she chose the latter, scuttled down the steps and began dodging a way homewards, reaching Mr Williams's just when police reinforcements brought up from Balsall Heath and Erdington were thrown in. Then the conflict really was joined, batons and bricks raining on friend, foe and onlooker alike.

"Go back, go back!" I screamed (although she could not possibly have heard me).

However I need not have concerned myself for, displaying a presence of mind under heavy fire which would have earned her the Major's admiration, she stretched both hands into the bookshop's window and, fishing out a massive *Times Atlas of the World*, employed this alternatively as shield and weapon. One monster, seeking to snatch her handbag, reeled from her blow to sink beside an overturned car, this doubtlessly being the first time the concentrated wisdom of the ages had made any impact on him. Then, as the tide of battle ebbed, this splendid person, after wiping its dust jacket with a handkerchief, carefully replaced the volume in Mr Williams's window. By this time I had reached her side to offer an arm and to warmly commend her valour.

"Thank you, dear," she said. "How kind of you to say so. But it was no more than my dear father would have expected of me. In fact, the last thing he said on Worcester Shrub Hill

Railway Platform as I left home for the first time, 'Never forget that you are a lady, Helen, Never!' And I never have nor shall. Just a moment, dear. . . ."

She stepped back to poor Mr Williams's gaping window and removed Barbara Pym's novel, *A Glass of Blessings*. "Ever since dear Lord David Cecil recommended this, I have been trying to obtain it from the Public Library but it was always out. But, as my dear father so often told us, 'There always is one grain of Good hiding in each stack of Evil'. And (stroking the novel) how right he was! Of course, I shall return it when Mr Williams opens again on Monday. He will understand."

By now the rioters had rallied to throw back the police who (lacking the excellent early training of my new friend) had fled in less than good order. Even their superintendent abandoned his loud-hailer ('Hold firm you lads at the front') and took to his heels until halted by a new platoon bussed up from Handsworth, a notably tough lot recruited in the Black Country. These advanced menacingly, their first wave banging upon plastic shields whilst following ranks held theirs above their heads – an interesting and impressive re-creation of the Roman Army's testudo.

But, clashing dustbin lids, the yobs still came on until, like medieval armies, both were locked in hand-to-hand combat.

And then I spied Matthew.

It was his custom to lead the choir in procession down the main aisle, then through the west door, out round the south side's exterior and thence back into the vestry. Now, emerging from the porch, he was brought face to face with his erupting mission-field. And halted in astonishment. But for no more than a moment. Turning to wrest the ornate Sir Ninian Comper-designed processional cross from Old Father Time (his Verger) and holding it on high, he plunged downstairs into the heat of battle.

Then, when he had buffeted and bashed a way to the middle of the road, like a lollipop man he raised a free hand to halt the police whilst presenting his cross at the other lot. It was the most dramatically stupid act of valour I shall ever witness.

I was not the only one to gawp. Hubbub and bricks diminished and a great silence reigned. (If ever there was a time for the Angel of Mons to reappear, this was it.) Then he lifted up his voice and cried passionately, "My house is the House of God and ye have made it a den of thieves." Which was hardly fair on the City Police.

But this bizarre interlude was momentary. In fact, the screams and drumming rose to a new pitch of violence because, not unnaturally, this pronouncement had incensed both sides. And down he went and once more the battle was joined over him.

But then there was a most extraordinary intervention. The rest of the Procession, who, in great dread of spirit had huddled in the porch, thus penning in their following congregation who suddenly burst out like a cork from a bottle and poured tumultuously down the steps to their pastor's succour and, under covering fire from a rain of hymn and prayer books hurled by choir boys, set about both mobs.

This flank attack (as students of our island story, recalling Colonel Ireton's ambushed dragoons at Naseby, will understand) confused the issue and both lots drew back in baffled disorder. Thus, with Father Time dragging one ankle and the Choirmaster the other, Matthew was pulled clear of no-man's-land and laid out under the porch with a beautifully forgiving smile smeared across his theatrically bloody face.

"Hetty, dear," he murmured, "Be kind enough to mention to Mrs Gilpin-Jones that I shall be late for supper and will she keep it in the oven. I shall remove it and take care to turn off the gas before going to my room."

His air of fortitude much impressed me and I thought, Well, if this is how these Christians can face adversity, perhaps I shall overlook Ronnie's cowardice and give them another try.

I should like to have reported that his disciples, having saved their fallen leader, then regrouped and, singing *Onward Christian Soldiers*, surged once more to the attack. But they ignored their Curate's feeble cries, "Where is the Cross? Where is the Cross?" And Father Time, cleverly anticipating likelihood of nomination as a paid official to pluck Comper's brand from the burning, declared that it already was lodged in the choir vestry. Whereas, even as he lied, I glimpsed a Muslim warrior scything a swathe through the police with it.

Then I hurried homewards by side street and towing-path to report that I had failed to stop the riot which we innocently had initiated outside our house and in our front garden and that Matthew would be late for supper.

Stage-struck

The riot died down as swiftly as it had blazed. An ambulance and a mortuary van cleared away its two unwitting authors and the Corporation Public Health Dept. swilled down the drains blood from our fronting pavement. In fact, but for a charred smell, no one in Archdeacon Street need ever have known what had spilled over our borders during the darkness, and there really was no need to gaze aghast at gutted shops, blank-eyed terraced houses or the youth club where, so I heard, a pair of teenage lovers had been incinerated.

And anyway, my first and last visit to a music-hall drove much of that dreadful Inner City night from my mind. When Ted invited me to accompany him, I thought to stall the issue by insisting Mrs G-J be asked too. Of course he was miffed but, recognizing that I was adamant, called my bluff and off the three of us went.

"Not my cup of tea," she whispered. "Opera and RSC are my style but, once he'd bought the tickets, I didn't want to hurt his feelings: the Working Class are so touchy. And he does pay his rent on the nail." Then, as we looked around the scattering in the pit, she added, "Just take a look at their dead faces and their awful women scarcely fit to waddle for fat." She drew in a dramatically worldweary sigh. "Yet once they were bright eyed kids."

I was unprepared for this philosophy of despair. Is her assessment subjective or objective? I asked myself, this method of cold-eyed scrutiny having been recommended to me by Miss Braceburn.

"Well – say something, Hetty," Mrs G-J hissed. "Don't just sit there looking such an insufferable bookish little prig. Can't you just see them down their burrows, munching, snoring and copulating?"

"Yes," I replied guiltily, "Yes, indeed I can, Mrs Gilpin-Jones. "And I suppose that someone has let them up for air just for the evening."

This mollified her. "Fancy finding yourself here in Fishfingerland and stuck in a corner with one of them at a party," she went on. "You'd have to be double-drugged. Though (to be fair and I always like to be that), I don't suppose they have parties and, anyway very few folk of even our own kind have gaiety of spirit enough to conduct a conversation with strangers unless they're tanked up with booze. Family parties are different: venom replaces gin as lubricant."

Then the curtain went up and one act came tumbling after another. Rabbits peeped from top-hats, doves fluttered upon shoulders, small women were heartlessly tossed hither and thither, a pony danced, grinning women appeared balancing on balls. And brief bouts of inane chatter tied one tired act to the next.

'Bang, bang!'
'Hey, you've shot my wife.'
'I've shot your wife?'
'Yes, you've shot my wife.'
'O.K. Have a shot at mine.'

We endured glumly.

At length, a couple of weary old jossers tottered in with a legless tabletop and upon it swooped a couple of roller-skaters. They whizzed about like mad. It was yet another revelation of what human beings will do to make a living.

"What an odd employment to take up," Mrs G-J whispered. "Do you suppose they learnt it at night-school?"

They stopped as suddenly as they had started.

There was no applause.

The man came to the edge of the stage and peered into the gloom.

He wore a glad smile. "Will any member of the audience please step forward and join us on the stage?" he called.

No one did. Even I, who had never before visited a theatre guessed what happens to members of audiences who step forward: they either are half-killed or exposed as half-witted.

"Please!" he begged.

He might as well have addressed a brick wall.

"It will be O.K." he pleaded. "You won't have to do any-thing. Mave and me just would appreciate a teeny bit of help with our act."

"In *Girls' Own Paper* they always showed a man in the wings with a big hook to drag off flops," Mrs G.J whispered.

"We only need a little co-operation," he cried despairingly.

I was not unmoved by this cri-de-coeur, recognizing that this was the climax of the act. I therefore pressed against the back of my seat and closed eyes and heart. This latter however would not stay shut so I hacked Ted's ankle and suggested that, as our host, he should go and help the poor chap.

"Me?" he muttered incredulously, adding smugly, "Think I'm daft?"

"Please!" the roller-skater cried plaintively.

"Oh please!" his mate echoed.

"Whatever is wrong with you, Hetty?" Mrs G-J whispered crossly. "For goodness sake do stop that moaning. Please do take your hands from off your eyes. And sit up."

How could I explain that I was suffering intense spiritual anguish, that I was seeing the wretched pair being handed their cards by the theatre manager, hearing his brutish refusal to recommend their act to other theatres, witnessing them, shoulders hunched, traipsing jobless to their cheerless lodgings, him cursing, her in tears. Someone *had* to join them on the stage.

"Oh God, do not let me leave this seat," I prayed. "Oh dear God, send forth Another."

"Hetty!" Mrs G-J hissed. "Hetty! Do stop that keening noise. People are beginning to stare at us. And for goodness sake cease that rocking. Is it your tummy?"

"Please God, please! Not me, not me!" I moaned. "Or at the very least, make Mrs Gilpin-Jones restrain me."

"Wherever are you going?" she snarled furiously. "Sit down, you ridiculous creature. This is absolutely the last time I shall accompany you anywhere. Even to church."

She snatched at me. But I already was staggering down the

gangway, unsteadily gathering speed on the slope, reeling from one row of seats to the other. And still moaning. If, later, it had been reported that I was foaming at the mouth and with my eyeballs turned up, I should not have disputed it.

Never shipwrecked mariner spied a distant sail with more joy than that roller-skater watched my terrified progress.

"Ah, here comes a good sport," he cried gratefully and, fearing that my legs might give way before he had me in his clutch, added, "Give this gorgeous young lady a big hand, folks."

"It's this way, dear," his wife hissed down at me through clenched teeth. "You can't crawl up there. Nor there! Nobody can. Here! This way!" And she bent over and guided me to the steps.

But when I reeled on to the boards, although still maintaining a glad smile, the man muttered harshly, "Thank God, Mave. But look at her size. A ten-stoner and close on six foot. . . . Just our luck. She's too much for you to handle, love. I'll have to do her." Then, willy-nilly he spun me round so that my back was against his chest and then inserted his arms beneath my armpits.

"Listen Miss and for pity's sake stop that moaning: Nobody's going to kill yer. *Listen you stupid creature.* Just stay still and lean on me. Got that? Just do that and-you-won't-get-hurt. Got it stupid?"

We began to gyrate. At first my heels scraped round and round the tabletop. But, as he picked up speed (whilst still staying on the same spot) my legs lifted and took off, until, at top speed, I was whizzing like a helicopter propeller and knew why, now and then, one flew off. In a mild sort of way, during Miss Lindsay's physics lessons, I had heard of centrifugal force but now knew its blind terrifying power. For, as my grunting partner drove himself to a new access of dizzying gyration, my body lifted above horizontal. Then higher! Where shall I land? I wondered. Front stalls, pit, dress circle, gallery?

It was much, much more alarming than say a ride in a cab of an express locomotive where, although the scenery rushes at you, it remains comprehensible. But now, painted back-cloth, Mave's smeared-on smile, props, wings, darkened house, merged into a terrifying whirlpool. And I had suspended appeals to God who, yet again, had let his child down when, with death without pain my last hope, speed slackened, my heels scraped, we sagged to an earthbound stop.

Well, of course, I could not stand. I still reeled in dizzy circles until I fell flat: the house howled. We had been the crashing hit of the evening.

But when I collapsed into my seat there was no hero's welcome from Mrs Gilpin-Jones. "Oh you silly, wilful extrovert," she hissed. "Oh, if only I had known it when you came to my door! Douglas or no Douglas, I would never have taken you in. I just pray no one who knows me is here. No wonder your poor mother gave you away."

But Ted was staring as though he had never seen me clearly before. And, as we made for the exit, he whispered, "Magic! You were big magic, Het. Better than Desperate Dan! Or Popeye! Next time I'm near that gallery, I'll give them painter chaps another go. After tonight, what suits you, suits me. Het rules OK."

But Mrs G-J's just appraisal had hit its mark for, as she hurried us homewards, I knew that she was right − for whom but one with a dangerously serious defect of character would so have exposed herself to private danger and public ridicule? I had not wanted to go. And yet I had.

Did my real mother spot this likelihood within hours of my birth? Or had the NHS psychologist put me on a diagnostic

97

machine and warned her to palm me off upon someone else just as quick as she could? I saw him sitting there in a white coat and looking grave whilst my mother peered with alarm at the bundle on her lap. 'Ms X' he would have said in tones of compassion. 'That child will be a prey to unpredictability to the end of her days. Anything, anything could happen. This is a solemn warning. Before going to bed, all knives and blunt instruments must be locked away. She may appear as she is now, as good as gold, but mark my words and mark them well – the poor little mite is Under Compulsion. Before it is too late, give her to a couple better able to protect themselves.'

Mrs G-J, still speechless with suppressed indignation, grimly let us in and flounced off. I shook off Ted and sagged dispiritedly upon the hall chair, hoping that the longcase clock's comfortable ticking would settle my nerves. ("I always so admired you, George," Miss Foxberrow was saying. "Oh why didn't I confess it! That afternoon you took on that vile bully, Billitt, oh could you not see that I would have done anything you asked? Anything! Anything! But the moment passed. . . . It was Cambridge did for me. All head, no heart! No heart!")

And she began to weep.

These heart-throbs of maudlin regret only made my condition more desperate and I fled to the Second Floor. What a pair of chumps you were, I thought savagely. You and your George! It only needed one or the other of you to have flung open a door and to have entered in your pyjamas, announcing boldly, 'Here I am. Move over. I cannot live without you. Do not bother calling for help. I shall not leave till you are in my arms and have agreed to a longstanding arrangement.'

As if in sympathy with these sentiments, Mr Peplow struck up, " 'Not a drum was heard. Not a funeral note. . . .' "

Then, in the darkness, I understood that he and Miss Foxberrow had not utterly bowed before adversity. By day each had retained carryovers from an imperial past: it was only at night, in the darkness that they surrendered. And this recognition that others had outfaced fate yet come off in good order, comforted me and did much to slough off the day's disaster. So I fell asleep.

I am forgiven

Next day, Mrs Gilpin-Jones had got over it. "It is no more than a slight defect in your make-up. Nothing needing professional help," she explained. "We all have them — although yours seems to take a more violent form than most people's. If ever again you feel things are getting on top of you, you are to let me know immediately. For goodness sake don't do anything irreversible — jumping into the canal, lying down before a railway engine, that sort of thing: this world can be a joyful place.

"And I'm deeply sorry for what I said about your mother. Even though neither of us know her, I am absolutely sure that she didn't want to give you away. Particularly to that awful couple you have described to me. Now am I right — you came to Brumbrum to find her?"

I admitted this and she agreed that this was quite understandable and, in my circumstances, she would have done the same and went on to promise that she would ring around and discover how one sets about doing this.

"Not much luck, Hetty," she told me a couple of days later. "There seems to be half-a-dozen adoption agencies but friends tell me it would be easier to get out of Winson Green Jail than to get into their filing cabinets. And it would be as much as their jobs are worth for staff to tell who went where to whom. But I think you should reconnoitre one and see if you can discover a chink in the official armour. Here is the nearest address."

And that is what I did.

Looking for a Mother (1)

The office was in a district which had trees, detached houses and private schools. The agency itself was a redundant vicarage sulking in a patch of dispirited laurel bushes. In its vestibule a government health-warning: *SMOKING CAN KILL*, had been unofficially extended, *AND SEX CAN STUNT YOUR GROWTH*. There was the usual discouragement-office staffed by a sour woman whom I side-stepped by declaring my business personal, family in fact, and so was admitted to a sunny room with Monet's *Poppy Field* on a wall and a discontented looking woman beneath it.

"I suppose it's the usual?" she snapped.

"I don't know," I answered. "What *is* usual?"

Used as she was to enjoying the upper hand with which to brow-beat girls repenting their folly, my riposte upset her.

"When are you expecting?" she asked brutally.

"I am not expecting anything," I said, "although a little politeness would not come amiss. I am here hoping for help in finding my mother. You, of course, may not know her whereabouts but perhaps you will advise me how to begin looking effectively elsewhere?"

"Oh, so you are an adoptee," she said, lighting a cigarette and blowing smoke at me. "Well, you'll never find her. Such information is more than confidential, it is highly-confidential, it is Top Secret. And the reason for that is, although you may want to find your mother, let me assure you that your mother definitely will not want to find you. Not on her doorstep anyway."

"That is neither here nor there," I protested. "Surely every-one has a perfect right to know who her mother is. You know your mother, I suppose?"

"And that is neither here nor there either," she countered. "My mother doesn't come into it. Our circumstances, thank God, are utterly different. You have never known a mother, so how can you miss one?"

"Well, she knows me," I said indignantly. "I lived inside her for several months."

"You have lied your way into my office and I can see you are determined to be difficult," she said coarsely, rising from her chair. "And I am not here to be quarrelled with. You will *never* find your mother. You are part of her past. If she hasn't forgotten you, you can bet your life she'd like to. Like it or lump it." She touched a button and a big commissionaire came in.

"Show this young trouble-maker out, Mr Cascob," she ordered. "There is nothing that can be done for her and she should not have been allowed to disturb me in the first place. Send the receptionist to me."

"I shall write to my M.P." I cried.

"Come along, dear," Mr Cascob advised and, when we were back again by the front door, he continued, "You're not the first, Miss: we have them all the time seeking their mums particularly when they get in the family way. But they all get the same dusty answer."

He patted my arm. "I am a Barnardo-boy myself," he told me. "And so I know how it is. Though actually I found mine. And wish I hadn't." Then, as I already was well on my way to the road, he called cautiously after me, "There's Neville Chamberlain House you know, dear. Everybody born has got to be put down there. It's the Law."

"Of course!" Mrs Gilpin-Jones said when I told my story. "Of course! Naturally! We're all down in some register or other till we snuff it and they draw a red line through us. Mmmmm – I can see possibilities in your kind Mr Cascob's

102

hint. Let me brood on this, for such an expedition will be hazardous and must be well-planned. Just up my street, in fact. I rise to a challenge. Hetty dear, are you happy here with me?"

"Oh yes!" I answered. "I am, I am very happy here with you, thank you, Mrs Gilpin-Jones."

The Slave-Chain

Ever since my humiliation in the music-hall, I had become ever more magical. Each morning as I served breakfast, Ted looked hungrily at me. Who knows — perhaps I may have been as appetizing as the sausages. And, at our evening meal, during the shepherds' pie (a skill which I had picked up after no more than a single lesson at a nearby night-school) he became jealously miffed at any intellectual repartee between Matthew and myself or any reminiscence of the heroic part played by the curate during the riot (which already had passed into local folk-lore). "If I had been there I should have done the same, Hetty," he muttered. "Except I wouldn't have dropped that cross: I'd have felled someone with it."

I now knew what Mrs G-J had meant when she classified him as demoniac. Despite striking physical similarities to Neanderthal Man, his path from Tubes apprentice to Presidency of Confederated Industries and a knighthood was as fixed as the stars in their courses. And he was going to be very, very rich.

One evening, as he convoyed me from my cooking class (across the borders of the Inner City), he was complaining peevishly at my refusal to accompany him for a weekend in Kidderminster. "It's a posh B&B," he was saying, "and they pile as much on your plate as you can get down you and you can always ask for some more. I should have thought you'd have liked a break from cooking and washing-up." He looked unbelievably besotted. "And the woman who runs it is really broad-minded," he added.

"Well I am narrow-minded," I replied. "Whoever wants me must marry me. I shall go to the altar or grave pure as driven snow."

"But these days nobody gets hitched without a trial run," he protested. "Things have moved on since your grandma gave you that crap. If you keep it up you'll end gathering dust on a shelf."

"Moved!" I exclaimed indignantly. "Moved which way? Back or forwards? And, as for the shelf, the prospect sounds marvellous. Books live on shelves and I probably shall have written one or two to join them before I am taken down and dusted by some man who can wait for a good thing when he spots it." (Browning's apt words along these lines would have been wasted on him.) Instead, taking advantage of a passing street lamp I off-handedly gave him a double eye-flash.

"You're magic, Het," he moaned.

But captains of industry do not give in easily and, as by this time we had reached no. 27, he earnestly asked to be shown exactly where in the shrubbery the second man had shot himself. It was Elementary Decoy Lesson One and I fell for it. He immediately got a grip on me. "I wish you would open your mouth when I kiss you," he grumbled. "I'm not your uncle. And try pushing your tongue out. Oh well, never mind. Look, I've got you a little present."

"I cannot see it here," I said, similarly resorting to guile, whilst slipping past him doorwards. He followed and thrust an enormously heavy parcel at me.

"And pray, what is this?" I asked, tearing it open. "Some sort of adornment. That I can see. Whereabout my person do

I dangle it?"

"Dangle it!" he repeated stupidly.

"Well, am I not to hang it somewhere? It is unusually long for a necklace. Or can it be to secure some fierce animal? I could not possibly wear it; light sleepers would complain of its chinking and clinking as I went around the house. Tell me – for God's sake, what is it?"

He looked past my head and muttered guiltily that it was a slave-chain.

"A slave-chain?" I exclaimed incredulously.

He nodded miserably.

"And when am I to have its ancillary? At Christmas?"

"Ancillary?"

"Yes. The ball – for my ankle."

"It doesn't have a ball," he said, warming to the possibilities of a discussion on mechanical detail. "You just put the chain round your waist and fasten it with that little brass padlock. To show you are mine."

"Your what?"

"Well, you know. . . ."

"I don't. And I am not yours. Since leaving Jordans Bank, I have ceased being anyone's. I am now a Free Spirit. Here, you chump, take this back to the ironmongers (or was it the pet shop?) and ask for your money back. Say it would not fit your dog's neck. And now you can buy me some fish and chips and, as we stroll along, you can tell me all about your Mum. I suppose that, like almost everyone else, you had one?"

And that is what we did.

A comprehensive defeat

Life in Mrs Gilpin-Jones's establishment was not one of that earnest strife and endeavour sternly recommended to Waterland High's Upper Sixth by Robert Browning and things strolled along come-day, go-day. I had not experienced before the joys of not needing to fulfil myself nor known that life as a birdbrain can be bliss.

So I happily toasted, dished-up and dusted my way through that hot August until September came with an autumnal restlessness brought on by mild airs, mists, mellow fruitfulness and prospectuses falling through letter-boxes promising that by conscientious attendance on Tuesdays and Thursdays (7-9 p.m.), when spring came one would be talking enough Italian not to be overcharged in Venice, virtuously appreciative of Schoenberg's musical offerings, able to leap into the Kirkby Malzeard Sword Dance whenever one chanced upon it or imbibe enough Philosophy to put up with other human beings.

This mood of optimism infected Mrs Gilpin-Jones too. "It is time you looked around for a proper job, Hetty dear," she said. "Much as I like having you around for our little chats, of course. And, anyway, you can lend a hand in the evenings to cover your rent. So I shall find you a teaching post."

"But I have had no training," I protested. "And I don't have a degree or certificates. Surely, even these days, one needs something to show somebody?"

"Oh!" she laughed, "My friend who works in the E.O. tells me they will take whoever turns up at an Inner City comp. She says the casualty rate amongst raw recruits is horrendous. She says they'll just about shoot their teaching-finger off to get drafted back to base. But the line's got to be held somehow. I'll ring my friend and tell her you're going up to Cambridge.

"But I do not know yet whether I shall even scrape into a poly," I protested.

"My friend won't ask awkward questions," she replied smugly. "She'll simply tell her boss what I tell her and, if need be, improve on it. We were girls together at the last boarding-school I ran off from and she came to both my weddings."

And she was right. A couple of days later there was a tele-phone summons to the Charles Bradlaugh Comp to stand in for a Mr Lamplugg who had reported that he had suffered an accident doing something.

"You can't go dressed like that," Mrs G-J said. "You look like a pupil yourself. Here, you can borrow my heather tweed suit. It's a bit antique as well as too broad in the beam but we can safety-pin you into it. And there's my leopard skin three-quarter-length that Douglas shot. Your generation can wear anything and, who knows, it may have sneaked back into fashion. Anyway, if you have to run for it, camouflage might save you. . . ."

And, thus accoutred and looking as worldly-wise as seemed appropriate to the circumstances, I presented myself at the institution.

"The Headmaster!" a young man (I found wandering in a corridor) exclaimed. "You've got a hope: I've been here a term and have only set eyes on him once and I doubt if he knows I work here. Nor the Assistant Head – they'll both be fighting yesterday's battles in crisis-conference at this time of day. Who did you say you're here to sit-in for? Lamplugg? Never heard of him. Ah, here comes Hobson: he's been here longer than me."

"Lamplugg?" this chap said. "Name rings a bell. Lamplugg? He's either the little man with a bald head or that man

107

who . . . no, it can't be him; he's in jail. What for? The usual! Did you say he teaches English? Yes? In that case I'm pretty sure he's Lamplugg. Take her on a T-Wing and ask someone to direct you from there."

"T Wing?" my guide exclaimed. "That's not the Security Block is it? She says she's never done any teaching before." But Hobson already was gone about his business and in T Wing I was passed on to a harassed looking middle-aged man in corduroys who pushed me into a classroom. "This is Lamplugg's little lot," he said. "Don't expect too much from them, then they won't expect too much from you. You'll find some books in the cupboard. Lamplugg hides the key on a hook behind a radiator: pretend to lean there and then grope for it so they don't see you. Dish out plenty of house-points: that may work with some of them. Do not send any-body to me or, for that matter, to anyone else." He looked appraisingly at me. My leopard-skin did not deceive him. "You're only a youngster yourself," he relented. "If you like, at the end of the day you can tell me how it went."

The row did not abate as I was briefly inspected and doubtlessly assessed as unlikely to give trouble. The cup-board surprisingly yielded up a pile of Robert Brownings and these I dished out. "Quiet!" I yelled and, astonishingly, they were. (Well so are gunfighters before the shots ring out.)

"Page 67," I said, "Turn to page 67" and, anticipating the cease-fire would not last long, wrote it on the blackboard, adding, *Karshish, an Epistle.* But, even as I wrote, I knew that it would be beyond them. "No," I cried, "Turn to page 93 — *How they brought the Good News from Aix to Ghent.* Who made that noise?"

"Leila," a girl in a front desk giggled. "It was Leila farting. Her Dad won't grow nothing but artichokes down his allot-ment. She didn't fart on purpose, did you Leila?"

"No," Leila agreed and did it again.

"Let's read it in chorus," I shouted above the impudent laughter which greeted this non sequitur, knowing that there is nothing like noise to drown noise. "See yourselves a-horse. Galloping wildly through the night! Ready! Go! 'I sprang to the stirrup. And Joris and he. . . .' And it worked. 'Dirk galloped, I galloped (the class galloped). We galloped all three.' "

"Well, I think it was daft," Leila commented. "Riding like hell and doing in the sodding horses."

"And why couldn't they just ring up and tell them the Good News?" asked her companion.

"And anyway, what *was* the Good News?" Leila asked relentlessly.

I had never before considered this and admitted that it was a good question which I was unable to answer so she could have a house-point.

Somehow I struggled through to the bell. As they fought their way into the corridor, Leila paused to say dispassionately, "I can't see you lasting long. And you can stick that house-point up your fanny."

But a sad little girl hung back. "I thought it was beautiful, Miss," she said. "But not that poor horse dying. I'm going to learn it off by heart. What shall we have tomorrow? And I wish I had red hair like you, Miss."

"There is the one about a French boy who took similarly good news to Napoleon at the Siege of Ratisbon and then fell dead."

"Smashing!" she said. "Great! But why do they always have to fall dead?"

(She disappeared into the mob before I could give her a house-point.)

Eventually four o'clock came and with it a realisation that I was not up to life in a comprehensive: Waterland High had neglected the required battle-training. So I ran to earth the man in corduroys: he looked dead-beat too.

"I shan't be returning. I think that. . . ."

"Don't bother," he said ironically. "And I wouldn't myself if it wasn't for the wife and kids: they have to be fed. You did very well to last the day out. I'll tell somebody that you've been and then you'll be paid. Perhaps I should have your name and address. . . ."

On my way out a hand touched my shoulder. It was Leila. "Didn't I tell you?" she said and gave me what for her passed as an affectionate grin. "Give the Youth Opportunities a go," she advised. "Or go on the Game. Up the Hagley Road is the best pitch. With that hair you'll start a kerb-crawler jam. Sorry about messing you up in class but Robert Browning isn't one of my problems. Acne is."

Mrs Gilpin-Jones was not so exasperated at my tidings as I had anticipated. "My friend says the Education Office calls that School the bourne to which no traveller returns. What about trying that Youth Thing: my friend says it's the Council's new way of employing social-workers they can't sack."

Youth's Opportunity

I felt badly at being floored (as it were) in the first round. However, because it was necessary to put up with rigours of working for money, I swallowed my pride (always a choking business for me), and found the YO which was down by the canal in a chapel the Methodists had pulled back from. Naturally there was a mob of loafers, and these had settled like starlings on every perch to yell obscenities at those of us daring to seek employment.

Inside, there was some sawing, chopping and hacking

going on but an amiable elderly man broke off to direct me to the Supervisor. ('First left down the aisle and sharp right at the pulpit.') Evidently I mistook the way because a reconstituted vestry was occupied by four or five girls knitting baby-kits. "This is Module Four B," their instructor told me, "– the Advanced Opportunity Maternity unit. Go back round the pulpit and see her, *the Expert*." (This set off loud and prolonged laughter.)

So I did and found myself in a snug little refuge and before a cross-looking young woman who, when I had written my name, address and age and was pondering how to complete *Candidate's Work Expectations?* said wearily, "Forget that. I shall assume you have none, because we only can offer three opportunities – elementary baby-knitting, allotment-hut construction and basic horticulture (which is tidying up senior citizens' front gardens on problem council estates)."

After my ball-point had remained poised for two or three minutes above her enrolment register, she looked up. "No?" she said, "They're not inspiring are they? Well, as a matter of fact, there is another project; it only came in yesterday and we need a superior candidate to pioneer and report on its work-absorption rating, so that I can assess how many other opportunity-seekers I can find opportunities for.

"It is dolling up headstones in St Tobit's Graveyard. Initially, since this is a Pioneer Project and thus does not rate a Module yet, you will have to find your own bucket and scrubbing-brush. But there is a tap on site and we will furnish detergent. If you put in the required hours we pay £40 a week."

Well, I thought, at least there will be no cheek and answering back to put up with down there. Furthermore, there will be some biographical reading, at any rate the basic facts – *'Natus est'* and *'Obit'*. "That will suit me down to the ground," I said. "And thank-you. You can rely upon me."

The deposed social-worker had cheered up during our interview. "Miss Beauchamp," she said, "I feel utterly confident that for once, we have fitted a square peg into a square hole. I rarely have superior candidates with ten O-levels present themselves. As a matter of fact, I have half a mind to give up this thankless administrative task and sign myself on. Cleaning up churchyards suggests limitless opportunities.

"Perhaps if, together, we can make a big thing of this, I might be asked to direct a National Headstone Project; there must be absolutely hundreds of thousands of them accumulated up and down the country waiting to be spruced up. And then I could recommend your appointment as Assistant Director. We could set up a Mobile Task Force, stay in comfortable hotels as we travel around . . . and so on. With all these dead lying around, it could be a lifetime's job for both of us."

She was talking with gathering enthusiasm as the glittering ramparts of dreamland rose above her drab surroundings. "No other Y.O. has such an Opportunity on its books. We shall be the flagship. Because much will depend on the initial impression made on St Tobit's vicar, you will dress conservatively won't you? And, if you play a portable it must be Radio Three. Never Radio Two! But I can see that you can be relied on absolutely, Miss Beauchamp."

So, leaving her luxuriating in this heaven-sent opportunity, I passed unscathed through the hammer, saw and hatchet zone and, emerging into canalscape once more, found Ivan getting enthusiastic cooperation from the gross oafs who he was posing before his camera in attitudes of eager but fruitless work-seekers. I took him apart.

"Ivan," I said coldly, "Listen good. True Britons not like this lot. True Britons have spunk. Tell Mr Kossov this. Also old folks at home in broiler-house."

"Spunk?" he asked. "Not know 'Spunk'."

"And, as for you, you foul-mouthed idle louts," I cried scornfully at my compatriots. "If we bought you bikes to get on, you would flog them for fags."

Matthew, who was doing his parish rounds, overheard this.

"Really, Hetty!" he chided unctuously. "What sort of attitude is that to take with these disadvantaged young people? Where is your charity? It is not as Our Lord would have spoken."

"No," I replied savagely, "He would not have wasted words like me. He would have taken a rod to their boneless backs."

And off I went, obscene abuse clattering about my ears and sealing the springs of charity.

A Ringing in the Ears

For some weeks Mrs Gilpin-Jones had been afflicted by ringing in her ears, some days louder than others. She was vague about its origin and could not be tied down to the year let alone the month when it had begun. "It crept up on me," she explained. "I didn't have it in Douglas's time so it either began during the stresses of my interregnum (I do not find widowhood easy, Hetty) or during Reg's reign, though it could have been brought on when he began wanting to come back – a sort of psychic signal . . . I have been told that no one yet knows what is the purpose of two-thirds of our brain area: perhaps the ringing comes from there."

It could not have begun when she found the dead man in the garden because she had complained of this ringing before, so perhaps she was right and Reg was at the bottom of it. It could have been guilt feelings brought on by Matthew who I now suspected was the friend she had been solacing when the door knob began to turn. But her doctor had pooh-poohed this. Indeed he had hurt her feelings by laughing loudly and by giving her a chit to take to the N.H.S. hospital.

"Do take a morning off work at St Tobit's and come with me," she begged. "The last time I attended there, the specialist did no more than blow into my ears and tell me to return in six weeks. And that was after I'd been kicking my heels for a good hour beyond his appointment time. This time I want a witness so I can complain to the District."

Despite its bedding plants, the hospital was a friendless-looking place. There was no end of notices, signs, slogans and directions and I felt that when some future archaeologist dug it up, he would report the site as a high security prison.

"Yes," Mrs G-J said, "they pour in more concrete each time they shut up another of those nice little cottage hospitals with geraniums in pots in the window, places where people know you and smile. Here, they hate us. Yes, yes, they do; I insist – the lot of them, clerks, doctors, nurses, ambulance-men – most of all consultants and their mates, the mortuary attendants. Don't laugh. Just you wait. Look – surely there's Ivan, our Ivan from no. 27, sitting like a lord over there by the Administration. Whatever is he doing here: he's not in a queue. He didn't say he was sick."

"Home-sick," I explained enigmatically.

We sat for a very long time idly scanning mags impregnated with other people's diseases, the sole diversion from a gallery of blank faces of similarly enforced loiterers. Now and then a bossy Scots sister poked her head out and called irritably for George Somebody or Beatrice Someone. Then, likely as not, a poor old lady would rise obediently and totter off towards the door. Eventually this woman called imperiously for Rose Jones and disappeared.

"Come on," Mrs Gilpin-Jones hissed, " '*Rose* Jones! This is absolutely the last straw." I could see that her blood was up: protest or caution was in vain.

Inside a Chinaman in his white coat of office was waiting (inscrutably of course) with an empty chair before him. But she spurted past him and homed in on a comfy little ante-room where the sister had flung herself into an easy-chair, rejoicing in freedom from subscribers wanting help. Her eyes were closed, so she did not immediately grasp the situation when Mrs Gilpin-Jones bent quite close to her face and said calmly but emphatically, "*Mrs* Gilpin-Jones."

"What? Why are you here? This room is private. It is not for patients. There are benches outside to wait on. How dare you! Who are you?"

"I am *Mrs* Gilpin-Jones. I am not *Rose* to you. I am only *Rose* to longstanding friends" (and turning towards me) "like you, Hetty." And rounding upon the sister she delivered a devastating, "And to my social equals."

She then withdrew and, drawing up another chair for me, seated herself squarely before the Chinaman.

But by now, the woman's brain had absorbed the message and she came at a run to level the score. "How was I to know that you were a Mrs or Miss. You might have been a child," she cried fiercely.

"My age must be on the cards you keep (even though you can never keep appointment-times)," Rose replied coldly. "Also my title. Neither we nor those others you keep await-ing your pleasure are intimates of either you nor this gentleman (nodding at the doctor). How dare you omit our titles. Let us have no more 'Georges' and 'Beatrices'. We employ you, not you, us."

This exchange of fire, not being in his native tongue, the Chinaman (by this time looking very much less inscrutable) was now twisting his head back and forwards like a Wimbledon Centre Court crowd until Rose put an end to the

115

unequal contest with a scorching ace. "Pooh!" she snapped. "Be off with you. Is there no work you should be doing?" And accompanied this with a dismissive wave.

She then turned upon the consultant.

"Well, here I am," she said. "But where is the gentleman I saw last time?"

"Ah," he replied, nervously rubbing the palms of his hands. "Thanks for coming (consulting his papers) Madam Gilpin-Jones. Very pleased. Mr Pettigrew-Saunders see only private patients. His list, my list today."

He then shuffled the file which must just have been dumped onto his lap.

"Ah!" he said, without conviction, "Mr Pettigrew-Saunders report you progressing very nice. Very nice! Very good! Please to return in exactly one month and we will have another look at you."

Rose turned red with rage.

"You are an out-of-work actor hired by the N.H.S. to impersonate a physician," she declared, leaning menacingly towards him.

" 'Come back in one month's time!' Is that what you tell each of the poor wretches waiting out there? You are as bad as her," jerking her head at his vanquished handmaiden who was growling uneasily within earshot. "I shall *not* return in a month's time."

She then bared her splendid teeth at this second victim but, to my great relief, withdrew to the corridor as another man, also in a white coat, sailed towards us and, because his eyes were unfocussed (fearing someone might signal for aid), he collided with Rose and started back. "Are you in charge here?" she demanded, stepping forward to re-establish body contact.

Being accustomed to having patients summoned before him and quite unused to being waylaid by one, he too had to

116

gather his wits before admitting that he supposed he was.

"Then pray why are we not addressed as 'Mrs, Miss or Mr'," she asked, pointing dramatically at the sufferers still staring phlegmatically into void but now with ears cocked. "Until misfortune caused them to reluctantly visit your institution, no one has called them Beatrice, Fanny or Harold since they were toddlers attending infant school."

"Well . . . yes . . . I suppose that would be not unreasonable. Not unreasonable at all," he nervously agreed, but learning from Rose's face that this was not enough, added, "In fact, it is an excellent idea. Thank you!"

He ridiculously supposed that this would end the encounter and began to edge a way round her.

"Then who is going to tell her?" she hissed, blocking his path and once more jerking her head at the now aghast sister, before once more thrusting it at him. "Me or you?"

He again muttered that he supposed he was in charge and that he had better 'do it'. Rose then stepped aside and, followed by the sister, he disappeared.

"Shall I go for Ivan and tell him to bring his camera?" I asked. "He could snap the scene for his Britain-in-Pictures Project."

The door opened. The nurse re-appeared and, her voice charged with venom, called for 'Mrs. Chalmers'.

Rose then leaned towards the waiting sufferers and, as though addressing idiots, enunciated very slowly, "Well, *someone* had to do it, hadn't she?"

The eyes of the bench-bound supplicants flickered momentarily but instantly resumed their peasant gaze at floor and wall. She looked bitterly at them, remarking loudly, "God help us, Hetty, this lot would have been just as happy under Hitler. 'Britons never, never, never shall be slaves' – Ha!"

These Britons still stared bleakly before them.

117

By now I had an uneasy feeling that, at this rate, the hospital would soon be strewn with her victims and it was time we withdrew before N.H.S. reinforcements overwhelmed us. "That is the way to the Exit," I pointed out.

"I am not yet done," she said. "And do straighten your shoulders: you are developing a stoop. And for goodness sake, shorten your stride, we are not on a healthy ramble through the countryside."

At Reception a girl approached us. "Yes?" she said thinly, "What do you want?"

"The Complaints Department!" Rose said.

"The Complaints Department!" the girl repeated, looked alarmed and backed off to a senior colleague who was sipping tea. I lip-read, "She says she wants Complaints. There isn't one, is there?"

"Not that I've heard of. Nobody's ever asked for it so there can't be. Are you sure it was 'Complaints' she said?"

"You're Senior Staff. You deal with it. It's your turn."

Senior Staff approached, smiling uncertainly.

"We don't have one. If we had one, why do you want it?"

"To complain."

"Oh, no one has ever complained before. That's why there isn't one."

Rose merely gazed implacably at her in silence.

"But I could find someone."

"Do," said Rose. "Meanwhile I shall remain here."

When she had subdued yet another sister flung into the breach by scornfully pointing to a label on her costume identifying her as *"Sister"*Jones and had hissed "Look at him" – he has *"Doctor"* Smith on his coat and here comes *Mr* Brown, the Consultant. Then why am I not *Mrs?"* and when we were back on the homeward bus I warmly praised her courage.

"It was no more than Mrs Thatcher would have expected

of any citizen of this once proud nation," she replied. "I take it that you are not a Socialist, Hetty? No, of course, you can't be."

"And Hetty – a word," she continued. "If you wait for Justice to descend from the mountain top, you will wait till not only your face but your bum turns blue."

We sat in silence for two or three stops.

Then she said, "So *THEY* (comprehensively netting every jack-in-office) refused to tell you who and where your mother was, did *THEY?* Well we shall see. We indeed shall see. Yes indeed we shall."

We journeyed onwards and, as we entered no. 27, she said, "Now here's a truly amazing thing – my ears are no longer ringing. I am cured. By faith and good works, I suppose." And she sailed triumphantly ahead.

But I paused by Miss Foxberrow's door.

"Oh George," she was saying, "Oh those happy, happy days we spent together at Tampling. Oh do you not remember poor Mr Pintle and silly Grace Tollemache and that donkey, Croser? What can have become of them? And what has become of us? Of us, George? Oh George, why can't we go back to the beginning and have it all again. Being young and in love, I mean."

And, as I toiled upstairs to change into my Y.O. kit, I knew that Youth was a very precious thing and thankfully, with Rose Gilpin-Jones as my guide that, more or less, I was making the most of it. If that is not a contradiction in terms.

Life in a graveyard

Being basically of a ruminatory inclination my new job was utterly to my taste.

Mr Palmer, my work-supervisor, recognized this and, as he left me, jocularly remarked that he could see I should not be lonely at St Tobit's. "Not with this little lot for company, Miss Beauchamp. And for all we know, they may be highly appreciative of your attentions, particularly you being a pretty young lady out of the top drawer. None of us relish being forgotten."

As I had foreseen, not only was there a mass of biographical material to read and reflect upon but, frequently, verse of an improving nature. Much of this doubtlessly would have been given the brush-off by the higher literary anthologists. Nevertheless it evidently had suited the tastes of parishioners at St Tobit's who, at their elementary schools had been reared on the lively strains of Henry Wadsworth Longfellow and Mrs Felicia Hemans. And, anyway, who ordained that the nominees of the Oxford University Press should be prime arbiters of taste?

> *Beneath this stone rests William Gunn*
> *Breathless he lies, his race is won.*
> *Beholder, thou too must haste away*
> *To breast that tape on Judgment Day.*

> *Erected by his sorrowing club-mates of the*
> *Birchfield Harriers*

For, in the end, what does worthwhile literary criticism boil down to but 'Would you personally dig into your pocket and buy the book?' And these St Tobitans not only had been ready to pay for their poetry but to dig really deep for it to be carved in stone (which comes a deal dearer than paper-print).

Although much of the verse surrounding me was addressed to the Almighty, I recognized this as artifice and that these exhortations were addressed to the executors themselves. Thos. Gray, of course, had got it dead right – my stones were teaching urban memorialists to die.

It was astonishing how many Brummies sought consolation, wandering around the scene of my labours. One old gent, Mr Meeks, came daily and far from resenting my intrusive presence, welcomed it. "Normally, there is nobody to have a word with," he told me, surveying his forefathers beneath the rugged elms and yew trees' shade (Thos. Gray). "So I have had to content myself with reading and rumination. You understand, of course, that many here are mates of mine, Miss."

As I accompanied him on a round of my Opportunity, he furnished intimate biographical detail to supplement that inscribed by the necropholists. He also pointed out the plot upon which he had made a down-payment. "Mind you I should like to have fixed myself up nearer my Auntie Nell," he confided. "I was very fond of her and she of me, which is more than I can say of my mother. Is that unnatural, Miss? And would you mind telling me your name, please?"

I replied that he could not have enquired of any person less qualified to answer, never having known a mother or of one not at all sure of a claim on any aunts – and that I was Miss Hetty Beauchamp. From that time onward he took an unusual interest in me, beginning with the comfortable news that mothers were not always what they were cracked up to be. He then warmed to a more technical theme – "Now then, m'duck, what you need is a brass-wire brush for it don't scratch stone like steel does. And that Vim they've given you don't come cheap. I'll have a word with the foreman who took my job at Croser's Copper Sheets and get him to find me a bucketful of mild abrasive and then we'll see what's what."

And this he not only performed but, knowing that there is

nothing so encouraging as example, put in a working-day on his knees by my side. Nay, more, for on the following day, he returned with a former workmate in tow, a Mr Cuzner, yet another of the discarded cadre of the city's highly skilled craftsmen.

Then, believe it or not, several more victims of compulsory redundancy appointed themselves to my staff so as to press forward our regenerative enterprise and Mr Meeks, Mr Cuzner and I considered it not unreasonable to encourage such volunteers to make a start on some uncle, aunt or half-remembered grandfather. And, feeling that we were engaged upon a more hopeful manifestation of national activity than the fraud, greed, rapes, riots, favoured by the media and by Ivan's Britain-as-it-is, I invited the latter to call upon us. Which he did, exclaiming that, in his country, my unpaid volunteers would be nominated Stakhovites, Heroes of the Revolution, and rewarded with free holidays by the Black Sea, dachas in pinewoods or medals permitting their wearers to advance immediately to the head of any queue.

But my work supervisor, Mr Palmer, unexpectedly coming upon my fellow toilers and revealing an unfeeling side to his nature, reported me to the Youth Opportunity Expert, bringing her at a run from her warm little vestry. To my dismay she also took up a reactionary attitude. "This work is not for them," she cried crossly. "Not a single one of this lot qualify under Section 19B. They are old has-beens pensioned off by the Government to stay at home. And doing it free is completely irrelevant.

"I shall request the Vicar to lock them out, Needless to say I am deeply disturbed by your Y.O. performance, Miss Beauchamp. What would be the result if this sort of thing spread nationally? You must order them to stop working and to return to their houses. Please remind them that there is a new Old Folks Club in Aston where they can attend a course on how to have a happy retirement and also be taken on subsidized bus outings to Stratford-on-Avon and Bourton-on-the-Water and, once a year (for regulars only) into Wales.

"My Head Office has now agreed in principle to extend this Opportunity to depressed areas in the North-East and for me to go up there and activate it. And now look what you've done. Just look. (She was close to tears.) You have put it all at risk."

Unfortunately, Ivan, who was quickly picking up capitalist customs, had sold a picture of us at work to the *Birmingham Mail* and this, with a chatty news story, came out that same evening. So that next morning many more old gentlemen and ladies equipped with their own cleaning-kit and packed picnics came even from as far afield as Wolverhampton and Kidderminster, beseeching me to 'set us on, Miss' and then fell to scraping and scrubbing like mad.

My superior was livid. "They are like a b****y swarm of locusts," she stormed. "Look at them eating up the Work. At this rate there'll be none left by the end of the week. You are at the bottom of this. I should have known you were a disruptive when I set you on. You have had too much education. You are sacked."

And wending my way homeward to No. 27, I ruefully decided that Education could be blamed for practically everything – whether you worked too little or you worked too much – and wondered if my ex-father, Mr Birtwisle, could have been right and if I should not have been happier living on in ignorance at Jordans Bank. I discussed this with Rose. "You have got it," she agreed. "In Britain, you can only be safe and successful by not making a song about it, so that people don't realize it's happened to you until the day after you've put your house up for sale and moved away to an olive-grove with adjacent vineyard in Spain. If the Socialists get in, it will be at least ten times as bad."

This I considered was going too far. And Mr Peplow agreed with me.

Breaking and Entering

The following Friday over a cup of cocoa, Rose asked me to tell her the story of my early life at Jordans Bank. "The bare bones of it I know, of course," she said. "Now fill me in with details, please." And when I had done, she told me, "Yours is a very affecting story, Hetty. Although you have not come off unscathed, many another girl would not have come through at all and this does you much credit. Even so, whatever is the sense of seeking out your true mother? What earthly help can she be to you now?"

"Well, for one thing, I should like to see what she looks like," I said. "Surely that is not unreasonable. She *is* my mother. How would you like your mind to be a blank about yours? Although I have not heard her mention it, surely even Miss Foxberrow must have treasured memories of her mum. I feel . . . well I feel that such a void must be bad for me — psychologically."

"But you might be so disappointed," Rose said gravely. "Why don't you just cut out a nice photograph of a *Vogue* model, put her in a little silver frame (which I shall give you) and think of her as your mother. A Surrogate I believe it's called. After all, you already have borrowed a name so you may as well go the whole hog and borrow a mother."

"However did you discover?" I cried. "Oh, how vexatious!"

"Easily," Rose replied. "When Ivan or Matthew or Ted ask you to pass anything 'Miss Beauchamp', anyone can see that it doesn't sink in for a moment. What *is* your name?"

"I haven't one," I said, digging in my heels and immediately uprooting them.

"Oh very well, it is Birtwisle."

"Who wouldn't change it!" Rose cried. "You stick to Beauchamp, dear. Unless, of course, you'd like to share my name. You could have either the Gilpin or the Jones or, for that matter, both. I've always found the hyphen helpful. And I'd be pleased to take you on."

I considered this.

"Thank you but perhaps No," I said. "I like you very much as a friend. Having you as a mother would change our relationship and maybe not for the better."

"In that case," she exclaimed decisively, "Since your mind is fixed on raking up what's dead and done with, let's do a daylight recce of that registry-place and decide how best to break in; then we'll do it Sunday night for the weekend is always the best time for uninterrupted crime, flood or fire."

"Break in?"

"Yes," she replied calmly. "How else can we enter? We shall be taking nothing but your own name and last known address. That can't be counted stealing; it's yours already. But if we have to break a window, then I shall leave a tip in their tea-kitty. Haven't you always wanted to break and enter somewhere? Now and then, when I feel like a half-boiled cabbage, I know that some mild danger would do me far more good than tablets."

And so, at nine p.m. on Sunday, dressed in a couple of Ted's boiler-suits dredged from the wash-basket and with a wrench and screwdriver from his tool-kit, we casually made our way through deserted streets to the registry. "I'm almost sure this is the spot we settled on," she said, peering at the spray-can art on the wall. "Oh, what disgusting louts they are!" she exclaimed. "No, don't look."

BeanzMeansFartz set us giggling.

We had no trouble at all; the inevitable lavatory window had been left open and, mounting a folding stool, we wriggled through. Evidently it had been decided that the building had a low burglary quotient, for the internal doors were either open or unlocked and a few moments later we groped our way into a bleak room furnished only with filing cabinets.

"Well, mercifully they're not computerized yet," Rose grunted. "Hand me that flashlight. Barnard . . . Barton . . . Bastin . . . Benson. . . . Ah, here we are. Binks . . . Birtwisle Bernard, Birtwisle Donald. . . . No Birtwisle Hetty, I'm afraid."

"Then try 'Ethel'," I suggested anxiously.

"Bingo!" she exulted. "There's not much about you but here's a photo. Is this you?"

I took the torch from her to examine an unpleasing baby and told her, No. Rosie took it from me, "Rubbish! That's you all right," she declared. "You had that hoity-toity 'I shall overcome' look even then. And here's your Mum's address. Oh, Sutton Coldfield indeed! So your grandad wasn't a pauper. Ah, here we are — *Wackley-Pitt, Wendy Maxwell, spinster, aged 19, no occupation.* That's all we need; you can keep the picture for your album; they'll never miss it. Quick — copy down the rest as I read it out and then I'll push the file back.

'Father — (unidentified) N.K.
Mother's father — Lieut. Col. R. G. T. Wackley-Pitt R.H.A.
(ret'd)
Child's name — None (unchristened)
D.O.B. — 20.9.1969.'

"There's someone else in the building," I whispered. Not far off a drawer was being forced; there was a clink of cash.

"We'll settle his hash," Rose murmured and yelled: "Collar him, George!" Immediately there was a panic-stricken clatter and someone, foolishly fleeing in the wrong direction, tripped over a chair and fell at our feet. Whilst we examined him by flashlight he scrambled up and cleverly assessed the situation. "Oh, you're in on it too! I might have known when I found the window open. Well, that's OK by me. I'm just here for the tea-kitty. Nothing else ever worth nicking in government offices now you can't flog typewriters."

"Nothing is safe these days with such as you about. Aren't you ashamed of yourself?" Rose asked sharply. "Why don't you find a job?"

"This *is* a job," he replied calmly. "A book I got from the library explained I'm an integral cog in the capitalist machine (which is all about moving money from one pocket to another). And turn that light either off or onto yourselves. Anyway, what about you? Just having a moonlight ramble?"

"We are redressing an injustice," I replied indignantly.

"And so am I," he broke in glibly. "A book from the library said. . . ."

"Oh shut up, you miserable pilfering windbag," Rose cried fretfully. "Let's go, Gladys, before he whines how deprived he is."

Without warning she switched off her lamp and must have given him a hefty shove because, as he fell again, there was a clatter of furniture and some pitiful groaning. Then she hustled me over him and, back in the corridor, switched on her flashlight until she found a *MEN*, pulled me in, pushed the plug into a basin and turned on the tap.

"Inner City vandals!" she giggled. "When they find a small flood they won't look any further than the drawer that oaf smashed and the desk he fell over. But, all the same, I hate to think of the stinker getting away with it. Come on."

When we reached the lavatory window Rose peered into outer darkness. "Mmmm," she muttered. "Your eyes are sharper than mine. Isn't that someone across the road? Don't worry – no one's going to spot you. That's right – push your head out further."

I reported that there indeed was someone trying to lose himself into a factory wall. "A right-minded citizen has noticed the window, and called out the Police," she said and, pulling me back, gave a flutey whistle. "Just to keep them on their toes; you'd never guess how hopeless policemen really are. They're not at all like those clever cops on TV."

By this time the Economics whizz-kid had picked himself up and we were able to chart his progress through the floods by his cursing when he met the tide flowing from the *MEN'S*. Then he must have fallen into the *LADIES* where he too turned on a tap.

"He's one of the nation's 99.5% who can't think for themselves and just latch onto other folk's bright ideas before striking for equal pay." Rose whispered. "Thus he deserves what is about to befall him. I suppose that I might as well turn off our tap now: it will be less on our consciences."

He stumbled past us and I heard first his shoes scruffing the lavatory pan, then the window rattling as he struggled out, and last, his plaintive cries as waiting coppers fell upon him. "For goodness sake, don't feel sorry for him," Rose scolded. "In gaol, they'll encourage him to take an Open University Course on computers so that, when he's released to prey on society again, he'll be qualified for robbery on a grander scale."

A blue light sped off and, taking our time, we dropped back into the street, brushed down our clothes and resumed our respectable roles in society. "Going off the rails is rather satisfying," Rose said drily. "Although, of course, one mustn't make a habit of it. On the whole, it's quite comforting to be trundling along the well-worn track once more, don't you agree?" and she nodded towards Miss Foxberrow's door.

128

"Do you remember standing up to that barrister, George," she was calling. "When the Government prosecuted you under that evil law? And that beery Mr Shutlanger! How he rose above his odious self to save you! Oh, George, what days those were! Oh why was I so wilful? 'There I'll be' you said — (your exact words) — 'and there will you be. And I shall be filling my pipe and you will be dandling our baby. And then I shall smile and you will smile. . . .' Oh George, the baby we never had. . . ."

"Now Hetty, do stop sighing," Rose said severely. "She knows very well you're listening: she has ears like a lynx and she is only spinning that yarn to put you off the scent. They topped him. She knows it, I know it and (glaring), for the last time, *you* know it. So let that be the end of it."

O Lord, I thought, as I climbed bedwards. A baby that never was now! I can't stand much more. I am going neurotic.

Next door, Mr Peplow was well into Corunna's aftermath,

> *We buried him darkly at dead of night*
> *The sods with our bayonets turning . . .*

Then his voice faded into sleep and, next morning, I felt quite cheerful again.

I find my Mother

"Well now that you have it, what do you mean to do?" Rose asked. "I mean that Wackley-Pitts name and address, for goodness sake."

"I should like to see her."

" 'See her' meaning 'seek an interview' or 'see her' meaning 'have a look'?"

"Only a peep! To see what my mother looks like. To see if she looks like me, for instance. Even a glimpse would be better than nothing. Then I shall feel easier and can forget her."

"You have a downright unhealthy outlook," she said. "You don't know how lucky you are not having a past."

"But I have a past," I pointed out, "Given though some of it was bogus."

Rose acknowledged this not ungraciously, for she was not one for stubbornly defending the indefensible.

"Then tell me how you'll manage this looking?" she asked. "To begin with, we can be pretty sure she's no longer at that address: either her People will be dead or she'll have married and moved away. I tell you what – let's go to Sutton this afternoon: I could do with a breath of rarified air."

So we did and everything turned out much simpler than we had a right to expect.

Rose had stuck a gummed label on a circular letter addressed to herself and re-addressed it to Lieut. Col. Wackley-Pitt, and, whilst I lurked a little way down the street of neo-Georgian mini-mansions (each in its tree-embowered plot), presented herself at the door of *Little Acre*, explaining that the letter had been wrongly delivered and hoped that it was not an important communication.

"It is not for us either," declared Mrs 'Little Acre'. "This is extremely kind of you (not many nowadays would have troubled), but the Wackley-Pitts don't live here. He passed away and his widow moved in with her married daughter, Wendy, although that was eight years ago (because I remember it was when we bought this house) and so she may have died also."

"Never mind," Rose assured her, "If you have an address and if it is not out of my way, I can push it through the letter-box."

"Oh we were given a forwarding address but the daughter's name is now Bond-Bulliver," Mrs Little Acre told her. "It should be in the hall-table drawer."

So, wreathed in smiles, uttering felicities of mutual esteem, they parted.

"I'm enjoying myself," Rose said, linking arms. "That was a very amiable woman; she was just my type and I should have liked her for a neighbour. Do you know, Hetty dear, I have come to believe that most of us become sick of being who we are or what life has turned us into. I find that telling whoppers and being someone else is quite exhilarating. I should have done it more often. But why do I need to tell you this: you're used to being just that. Not the lying part of course," she added hastily.

The address was that of another modern mansion. Tudor this time.

"First we must check that she is still living here," said Rose and, choosing a house six or seven doors further along, asked if Mr Bond-Bulliver was in and was told that he lived at the address we had been given.

"It's just a matter now of hanging about by this bus-stop," Rose said.

"We shall wait for the 48 or the 76A or whichever bus it is round here which never comes. Then we must trust to luck. I shall give her half-an-hour to go shopping or meet her children. If she hasn't shown up by then I shall have to leave you and go home to put the dinner on."

But, within a quarter-hour, fortune favoured my cause and, shopping-bag in hand, out she tripped, making straight for our observation post. "For goodness sake, don't stare," Rose cautioned. "I shall halt her long enough for you to have that last long look you keep bleating about."

"Ah, I'm so sorry to trouble you," she said, "But have you

any idea of the interval at which the 76A passes this way?"

Not many can lay claim to recall seeing a mother for the first time. Yet here she was – wrapped snugly into a very expensive dark blue alpaca coat with velvet collar, a pert black velour hat trimmed with a scarlet ribbon and tall Italian boots. But she was not so tall as me. In fact she was not like me at all – either in general or, with one exception, in particular. Her own oval face, peaches-and-cream complexion, natural ash-blonde hair. But my green eyes!

She glanced dismissively at me.

"No, I really couldn't say," she said in an out-of-the-top-drawer drawl. "Afraid we never use the buses."

She went on her way: she had not smiled.

"There you are," Rose said, "You can see for yourself that our walking clothes-horse is well stabled. ('We never use the buses,' she mimicked.) "I hope you observed her mare-like neigh. She's not your type, Hetty, and you certainly are not hers. Now you've seen her, you can forget her.

"Ah, here comes our maligned 76A. Let's go home and, if we pass her, it will be quite in order for you to thankfully wag a hand in hail and farewell."

A Visit from Polly

I had to put into abeyance an assessment of this extra-ordinary episode because, next day, the Major and Mariana came for the weekend.

"No more 'Mariana' please," she said. "After he and Gidner let me down in A-levels, any reminder of Tennyson is painful. From now forward I shall be myself – 'Polly'. Oh, Hetty, with you gone, Jordans Bank is a desert and I'm working on Grandpa to move elsewhere to end our days. I

132

say, isn't your landlady a corker! From now on I mean to model myself on her. We already have had two heart-to-hearters and she agrees that, when she was my age, in both build and disposition, we were alike as peas in a pod. The Major gets on tremendously well with her too: they're thick as thieves. I had the most awful bother uprooting him and then only on the understanding we stayed a couple of nights. But now he's shouting about being in no hurry at all to get back to Jordans Bank – and when shall we visit again. . . ."

This I could well believe because he already had found his way to Mr Peplow's attic and, cannonade by cannonade, was campaigning his way across the Iberian Peninsular. And quite touching evidence of this intimacy was his 'Hetty dear, would you be kind enough to visit a bookshop and to purchase for me the *Works of the Revd. Charles Wolfe,* making quite certain that it includes *The Burial of Field Marshal Sir John Moore at Corunna?* Flight-Lieutenant Peplow rates the poem very highly."

Rose too was not unimpressed. "The Major's a game old boy," she confided. "Brings to mind my dear papa. But I do wish he would move on from that Peninsular War: of course I do understand that he can't possibly have taken part in it but less well-informed persons, over-hearing him, might suppose him a great deal more elderly than he really is. I've told him several times there's a lot of living in him yet. But out there in those bogs you told me of (Jordans Bank! – What sort of a name is that!) and with only a chit of a girl for company can't be good for a man of spirit. Oh her heart's in the right place – I don't dispute that, Hetty – but I can't think she's much of a hand at the pot. Now is she?"

"No," I replied treacherously. "No, indeed, she is not, Rose. Far from it. Stew and rice pudding from a tin are what he has to manage upon. But he does not complain."

"Of course, the poor man won't complain. He's not the

complaining kind," she cried, rallying yet more strongly to
his cause. "No more than did Daddy. Their generation didn't
complain. They just soldiered on (as you might say). Oh that
Beveridge has much to answer for. He was quite as bad as
that Radcliffe-Maude who messed up all the counties so we
don't know where we are half the time. The Major's breed is
a dying breed . . . not that he's anywhere near dying.

"Ah, here you are, Major Horbling. I'm just going to brew
the cocoa. Sit in the armchair by the Aga and talk to me. I
simply can't wait to know what happened next on that
Torres Vedras Line. (We had just retaken the Forward
Redoubt.) And Hetty is just off to turn the beds, aren't you
dear?"

So the visit was a great success.

"You're sitting pretty," Polly told me. "Three chaps
buzzing like bees about you. Spare one for little me. Don't
bother saying No, because Ted's already invited me to your
local music-hall tonight." (And indeed Magic looked quite
furtive when I served breakfast next day.)

"How did things go?" I asked Polly somewhat stiffly.

"Oh, great! It was brill. He kept going on about me being
magic. And when a man with a circular-saw and a coffin
invited any member of the audience to step forward I'd like
to have gone but he forbade me. He said I was too precious
for what sometimes happened to people once they were up
there. What do you suppose he meant, Hetty?"

And I was not alone in finding their visit a not unblemished
success. Matthew was miffed too. "Mrs Gilpin-Jones is seeing
far too much of that elderly gentleman, don't you think,
Hetty?" he asked, apropos nothing in particular. "He's old
enough to be her grandpa. And if ever I set eyes upon one,
he's an out and out racist: he had the impertinence to ask me
if my father was a Zulu warrior and fought at Rorke's Drift."

Before they departed for Jordans Bank I learned that

Ronnie had finally settled on becoming a curate and that Lucy Gill had found a housewifery course at a poly and was wooing him hard with crème caramel, that Sonny looked utterly hangdog and near-suicidal and that Miss Braceburn and the gym mistress had gone on pilgrimage to John Keats' grave in Rome. And this news set me wondering if, after her John had died, Fanny Brawn had married another and, if so, after all those marvellous, marvellous letters from her truelove, she hadn't found her husband a trifle on the dull side.

I meet my Mother

When I told Rose that I was determined to meet and have it out with my mother, she took it quite calmly, saying, "Che sera, sera! Then you must look more a woman of the world and less the gawky schoolgirl. Let's go upstairs and see what's left of my gear when I was more or less your shape; there may be some rags which have survived Oxfam.

"Now you can't go in those black low-heels: they cry out in pain of a house-mistress church inspection. Definitely high heels; you must loom over her. And, for goodness sake, do stop striding like a ploughboy. Mince more."

"Oh Rose!" I cried, enjoying the fuss. "Don't be such a fuss-pot."

"There! Look at yourself. Let your hair flow. Toss your head – that's it; make it swirl. Surely you realize that it's your Essential Glory. And mince! Mince! That's better! Any mother, ignorant of that temperamental defect (which we have forgotten), would be proud of you."

"But I don't want her to be proud of me. I just want her never to forget me. I want her to squirm to the end of her days remembering me."

Rose laughed. "With that head of hair, she's scarcely likely to forget either you nor the chap who gave it you. When she's not squirming with envy, she'll be squirming with regret."

Rose had a wonderful way of injecting confidence into her frailer sisters. Quite up to Miss Braceburn's standards in fact (although, of course, lacking her stern moral tone).

And thus girded for the fray, I turned up at Sutton Coldfield. And waited. And willed her to come.

She did. But this time with two children, a girl and a boy aged about four and six and with an enormous Alsatian, all tripping jauntily along and making for the Park. As before, she looked fresh from the band-box; this afternoon the most notable features were a saucy straw-hat perched atop her piled-up hair, a scarlet wool coat and marvellous patent leather shoes.

"Shoo!" she cried gaily. "Off with you, Sarah! Adam, stay with Sarah. And on no account must Ponty be let off his lead."

Then she flipped a tissue, wiped a bench, seated herself, lit a cigarette and blew out a jet of smoke.

I approached, seated myself by her and murmured casually, "Smoking is injurious to the health. This is a government warning."

She turned fiercely. "How dare you! If you are not gone from here immediately I shall report you. I have seen you hanging about before. What do you want?"

"True," I said – "You have seen me before. And what do I want? Ah, of that I am not sure – yet. But I shall be wanting something."

She looked me disdainfully up and down. "You are being impertinent. Our Park is patrolled by attendants. Be off with you, and never let me set eyes on you again. Shoo!"

"I suppose that is what you said last time – as you hurried off," I said. " 'Never let me see you again.' "

I shall say this for her – she belied Rose's estimate of a low IQ. It must have been pretty high, for I could tell that she already had half-guessed that what she had hoped would never happen was happening. She stopped her silly protests and came right out with, "Who are you?"

"You know very well who I am."

"Who are you?" she persisted.

"I am your daughter, Mummy, your long-lost daughter," I

said and immediately regretted this melodramatic overtone.

She did not prolong a hopeless resistance: she was a tough customer.

"What do you want?" she asked brusquely, lowering her voice and quickly glancing to see how far away the children were.

"What do I want!" I said. "What about some belated motherly love. That would make a good beginning. No? Then perhaps I want no more than a close-up view of a ghastly woman who handed her baby over the counter like a bundle of unwanted clothes at a jumble sale."

That told.

The marvel was that, not for a moment, did it occur to her that I might have been an imposter. So I asked why not. She flushed and her lips tightened, plainly kicking herself for surrendering so easily.

"Well?" I asked again.

"Your face," she replied savagely, "And your hair."

"And this?" – pushing aside Rose's silk scarf. She glimpsed the little aquamarine and silver brooch Mrs Birtwisle had handed over. And turned away, dropped her head, tried to control herself.

"Oh you can gulp," I said coldly. "But what have *you* to sniffle about? You are very, very nicely placed. That anyone can see from your clothes . . . you have never had to wear them out like me. So blub away."

But if it was a performance, it was a very good one. She managed to choke herself under control. But only for a moment. Her sobbing began again.

"It is absolutely no use going on," I said. "You would be much more usefully employed deciding what you must do about me. Here I am and tears will not wash me away: when you look again I still shall be here. You threw me away like a cat in a sack. Well, I have crawled out of the pond."

"It wasn't like that," she protested with a show of spirit. "I wanted to keep you. It was my parents. Chiefly Daddy."

"My grandfather," I reminded her. And I do believe that this was the first time that she had considered him in this role.

" 'You can't keep it' he insisted. 'It has to go before you and your mother become attached to it. *IT HAS TO GO.*' "

(I became extremely indignant on hearing myself described as 'it'.)

"I cried all night (glancing at me as if she was afraid that I should disbelieve her). Next morning he did some telephoning and then Mummy and I were sent off in a taxi – in case the neighbours became nosey."

"Mummy and I and who?" I said bitterly.

"Who?" she sounded genuinely perplexed before tumbling to it. "Oh – And you," she added wretchedly. "By the time we got to the place both of us were weeping buckets over you. 'She has my eyes,' Mummy kept repeating *that.*"

"Did they inform you who had ordered me?"

"Not the exact particulars," she said. "They said it would be best for us not to meet: we might find it too distressing. They said it was a couple from a good Christian home who had been inspected by the Adoption Society so we needn't worry."

"They were called Mr and Mrs Birtwisle," I told her. "He was a spiteful rate-collector and she was his doormat. They also picked up a brother for me at another bargain counter: he was named Sonny."

"Sonny!" she said sharply.

"Not Nigel or Miles or Jonathan. Sonny!"

"Sonny!" she repeated as though the full horror of her betrayal had struck her.

"Perhaps you would like to know my name – what the Birtwisle's labelled me?"

She did not answer and it is only fair to say that, once more, her eyes brimmed with tears and that her lips quivered.

"They called me Ethel," I said indignantly. "Do I look an Ethel? What is my real name?"

"You hadn't one. I think one doesn't have a name until baptism."

"Oh, come off it. You must have thought of me as someone when you were carrying me."

"Well then – 'Sarah'," she admitted.

"Oh!" I cried looking indignantly at the children playing with their animal. "Oh, so she has been given my name!"

"But you needn't keep 'Ethel'," she bleated. "When you're twenty-one, I'm sure a solicitor can change it for you. I must admit it's not much of a name and I can see what you mean about it not fitting you. I don't suppose you need tell your parents. You can stay 'Ethel' to them and be your new name to friends you make elsewhere."

"Please stop calling the Birtwisles my parents. You are the only parent I have found so far. And, besides, I have left Osokosie and Jordans Bank and confidently expect to see neither it nor them again. But we shan't discuss that."

For a few moments neither of us spoke.

Then I said ironically. "My family is extending itself wonderfully; now I have a brother and sister."

"A step-brother and step-sister," she corrected me. "They had another daddy."

"So he didn't marry you? Why not? He must have found you attractive on at least one occasion; he cannot have sired me absent-mindedly. Did he not love you?"

"He said he did. And not just once. Several times."

"Well then?"

"He said we were incompatible. You wouldn't understand."

"Ah!" I remarked.

140

"It does happen," she went on, hopefully adding, "It may happen to you someday."

All this was extremely interesting for, on acquaintance, she was improving, modifying the bleak persona I had arranged for her. In fact we were becoming far too matey and it occurred to me that she might be a deal smarter than she looked: I should have to put the screw on.

The children brought our encounter to a natural end. "Mummy! Look!" they chorused. "Look!"

"What are you going to do?" she muttered.

"That I must consider. Yes, I shall need a little time to decide *that*. I may tell you next Wednesday."

"Next Wednesday!" she repeated wildly.

"Yes, next Wednesday, same time, same place. It is my half-day."

"But we visit his parents on Wednesdays."

"But not next Wednesday! If you are not here, I shall hunt you up and arrive by taxi to join the tea-party."

("Mummy, Mummy! Look!")

"Oh, you wouldn't!"

"Of course I would. It is not my custom to say one thing and do another. You be here next Wednesday, rain, hail or shine."

She gathered her chicks and set off homeward.

But the boy, Adam, turned back, approached menacingly and gave me a vicious kick on the shin. "I don't like you," he said. "Go away."

An Aristocratic Interlude

"My work done, Miss Beauchamp," Ivan told me a couple of days later. "Only one of Mr Kossov's Britain-as-it-is not crossed off."

"Let me guess," I said. "No, do not tell me. A dole queue half-a-mile long? Soccer fans murdering someone in the wrong scarf? An incompetent company chairman awarding himself a 200% rise?"

"Very funny but wrong, wrong. It is noble in palace. Much interest in my country. In my country have palaces but no nobles in them. Only ticket-collectors. There is palace open this day. Come. I pay bus."

Why not? I thought because, frankly, I had never seen a noble. The nobles of Jordans Bank had fled to Surrey several generations ago.

So we pushed off £1.25's worth deep into Warwickshire and, as the bus sped along I asked him about his mother.

"Not see Mamma much," he replied seriously. "Am Stalinchick. On the Sundays she came. Sunday no factory. Had big smile. Give me black teddy bear. Waits for me in Kiev."

"Your mamma or the black bear?"

"Black bear," he said.

The mansion was down a lane and only a half-mile from the bus route which was as well because it began to rain. A bedraggled little band huddled in the porch where we were stripped of our dripping coats and umbrellas. ('The carpets you understand. . . .') And, when enough of us had turned up, we were herded through endless rooms smelling of smoke, damp and decay. Our guide, a plump, amiable, vague person may have been the owner's wife.

"I think that is his great-great grandfather dressed as a hussar. Or could it be his great-great uncle? (They are *his* family not mine, you see. He becomes so irritable when I ask who is who.) This was the staircase someone or other was thrown down and broke his neck. The Wars of the Roses I think. Or was it the other staircase and the Great Civil War?

No (to Ivan) we have no objection to you taking snapshots for your album. The box for Overseas Missions is at the front door."

When we reached yet another room mourning its ancient glory, she put a silencing finger to her lips, halted our progress and disappeared into a further chamber. We heard sounds of one person trying to dislodge another and that other refusing to shift. So she returned and, raising her eyes to the ceiling (but, for once, not directing us to admire it) turned up the palms of her hands in a gesture of continental despair.

Behind her a very old man shuffled. Well, more than just very old: he was ancient.

"Is the noble?" Ivan whispered.

"Ah!" the old boy growled.

"Is the noble," I replied.

"Ah!" he growled again and for some tense moments surveyed us sardonically.

"Ah well . . ." he muttered, stopped, resumed his survey.

Some of us rubbed hands like so many Uriah Heeps, most of us looked terribly lower middle-class, all of us looked sorry for not only being alive but being discovered in his house.

He looked us over yet again.

"Ah well!" he repeated.

And turned away. We waited anxiously. He turned again.

"Ah well," he said dismissively, "I suppose you all voted Socialist."

Was Ivan's camera levelled to record this brutal affront? It was not.

And never again shall I set eyes on an impersonation of a True Blue Tory to equal Ivan's. Astonishing! So I looked once more and this time with admiration at the back of this old gent, my countryman, who, with a single basilisk pronouncement, had caused my companion to ditch his

143

revolting belief in the Brotherhood of Man.

"No wonder," I hissed at him, "that you cannot export your horrible Revolution."

Then a·door slammed, a key turned, a bolt shot.

"I am afraid that this concludes your visit," our guide said. "But we shall be open on Nursing Sunday next year. Please bring your friends."

Polly's Secret

"This time I have brought your cat," Polly said. "Percy was pining for you and, even though this Fenland season has been an unusually good one for mice, he grew skinnier daily. Look – now he has smelled you, he feels at home already. Oh you can't understand what fun it is to be back here after the tedium of Jordans Bank. As for Grandpa, he's been tugging at his leash, yet it used to be hell's own job dragging him as far as Wisbech. Coming here has speeded him up no end: he's retreated from Majuba Hill, embarked from the Iberian Peninsular, by-passed Neuf Chapelle and is regrouping his forces at Alamein. Give him a couple more weeks with your Mr Peplow and he'll be into that idiot Reagan's Star Wars."

Then, naturally, she had to hear about my search and, having long envied her mother's deathbed farewell, I made the most of having a colonel for a grandfather, albeit one heartless enough to have known me as 'It'. And she was notably impressed by my mother's wardrobe.

"She must have thought you a bit of a wreck in Mrs Gilpin-Jones's clobber of yesteryear," she remarked. "That leather garment – she must have worn it to drive in an open Dion-Boudillon on the 1912 London to Brighton. And don't bother giving me Old Man Browning's 'soul bursting –

earth's bounds' crap: except for you and la Braceburn and him, the rest of us form a skin-deep opinion of folk. Oh, here comes Ted." And she switched to over-drive, her eyes flashing on and off like Blackpool Illuminations.

"You're magic, Poll," he drooled. "Big magic!"

Utterly nauseated, I went.

"It must have been a sad day when you lost your dear daughter, Major," I yelled.

He did not take this in and I was gathering breath for another go when, looking puzzled, he shouted back, "Lost her?"

"When she passed away. That last sad day (as the sun sank)."

"What, is she dead then?"

"Your dear daughter – I am talking about her."

"When Hetty?"

"When what?"

"When did she pass away? She was here no more than a moment or two ago, bringing me this mug of tea and, as it usually is when she makes it – it's no more than water bewitched. So how can she be dead, dear?"

"Your daughter!" I shouted.

"Polly *is* my daughter," he shouted back.

"Her mother died. You can't have forgotten that autumn day – as the sun sank low."

"What is she dead then?"

(Heavens, it was starting all over again.)

"Yes, when she gave you Polly."

"She gave me Polly," he roared, sounding amused. "She gave me Polly all right. When she hopped it. 'Here you are,' the hussy told me. 'She's all yours now.' The last thing I heard she was in Dakota with that Yank top-sergeant and I hope she's giving him his fair share of hell too." And he began to laugh loudly.

And so did I.

"Does Polly know this?" I giggled.

He nodded.

"Then please do not tell her what you have told me, Major," I shouted.

"Oh no! No, oh no! Poll takes after her mother – she needs her dreams, poor love. But I hope they don't land *her* in Dakota. I read about it in the *National Geographic:* when it's not full of snow, it's clogged with dust. And nothing ever happens."

Then he became tremendously solemn (which was not his wont). "But we all need them, Hetty," he shouted. "Dreams! We all need our dreams, Hetty dear. Without them, some of us would go mad."

Rose falls in Love again

It soon became clear that it was not Brumbrum but Rose who had the Major in thrall: each keenly relished the other's company.

"He is an unusually well-informed man," she told me huskily. "As well as a very very good man. We have the most rewarding conversations you'd not believe. But I am so hoarse that I can't wait until Friday."

"Friday?"

"Yes, I've arranged for him to go to town to be fixed up with a hearing-aid."

She then looked more closely at me than was usual, before continuing, "You may as well know now as never that I have consented to become the second Mrs Horbling. But please keep this under your hat until he has broken the news suitably to Polly: I don't want any ill-feeling."

"Is he not a trifle too old for you?" I asked (meaning this as a reduced compliment).

"What has age to do with it?" she cried indignantly. "You don't suppose I'm planning to present Polly with a little brother, do you? We shall sleep in separate rooms and see how we progress from there."

"Are you not in love then?" I asked.

"Love!" she laughed. "Oh, for goodness sake, Hetty, do stop talking rot. He wants a friend to see him through to the end. And I want someone to confide in. And to cherish me. Large women need just as much cherishing as anyone else. Besides I need a protector."

"You cannot mean. . . .?"

"No, of course I don't mean what I think you mean. Don't be so absurd, you goose. I shall not be required to take to the street. We shall manage very well on his army pension and poor Reg's Gold Coast dividends. Oh Hetty, you are being very difficult this morning," she cried irritably. "And you are so naive: it is quite unbelievable. I suppose it's not having a mother. Why I even see that you didn't mean what I thought you meant," – for she had caught my eyes straying to the Major's cavalry sabre. "I mean that I need someone to protect me from Life's wear and tear."

" 'Be a god and hold me / With thy charms. / Be a man and hold me / In thine arms.' " I quoted, absent-mindedly taking down Robert Browning and dusting him lightly before pushing him back into the limbo of lost illusion. This literary aside was lost on her.

"Anyway," she went on, "Anyway, you'll be going off again to college soon."

"I rather have hope," I agreed, "But, at present, no more than hope. By the way, Rose, when you are married I am not at all sure that you will care for life in Fenland. Apart from Ely Cathedral there is not much there. . . ."

"Good gracious!" she interrupted. "I'm not going there: he's coming here and, for a time at any rate, things will go on much as before. It'll be just like having an extra boarder. And, by the by, the Major is very fond of you, dear, and we both shall want you to look upon our home as your home. After all, you and Polly are much closer than most sisters. And neither of us will ever forget that you brought us together."

She then relapsed into euphoria and, to bring her back to earth, I asked if she had told the Major about Reg wanting to come back.

"Of course not, silly. And neither must you tell Polly. Even though I know Reg is one hundred percent behind me. . . . After all, what has he to be jealous of? Haven't I made it clear enough to you that, unless the heating breaks down during winter, my future husband and I will not be occupying the same bed? At our age! The idea! Well, anyway, at *his* age! You are a funny girl, Hetty."

I suppose that she was right. And, anyway, once the Major had stowed his teeth into a tumbler for the night, if Reg did look in at no. 27, he would suppose him Rose's grandpa.

"I should have liked another white wedding," she murmured hazily. "White becomes me I always have been told. When Douglas and I wed, it was rather a grand affair — bells, lots of little choir-boys, top hats and tails, arch of swords, a bishop . . . the lot."

"Perhaps the Major could wear his medals and bring his sabre," I suggested. "In its sheath of course. . . ."

"It will be a very quiet do," she went on regretfully. "Matthew will do us early one morning at St Barnabas's. There will be just family. Well — Miss Foxberrow, even though she lives in a world of her own — she's been with me so long that she's almost family, worse luck."

"What about Ted?"

"No, not him."

"Ivan then. He should see an English wedding before he goes home. He may suppose we hold them in such institutions as People's Palaces."

"No, no, no," she said firmly. "If I had my way the only institution he'd see would be the inside of an English jail. I can guess what he's been up to with that camera of his."

"Well, Mr Peplow then?"

"He wouldn't understand what's happening. He's quite happy as he is – living on his memories."

This I felt was rather hard on my friend because I knew that he would know quite well what was happening and a wedding might be just the stimulus he needed to trip the points and switch him from the *Burial of Sir John Moore* to perhaps *John Donne's Epithamalion.* In this prevailing paradise, free now from dread of Mr Birtwisle, I rather should have liked to lie in the darkness and hear him announce,

> The Sun-beames in the East are spred
> Leave, leave, faire Bride, your solitary Bed . . .

However I did not mention this to Rose: she could be quite prudish about that sort of thing.

"But first, we will have a 300th Birthday Party," she announced. "Miss Foxberrow must be 75, Mr Peplow 94, Matthew I know is 37, Ted 20, you are 18, the cat is 10 you tell me and I am 46. It will also serve as our betrothal celebration."

"You have forgotten Ivan again," I said.

"Pooh! He hasn't been baptized so he doesn't have a birthday. They are hatched in ovens, then reared in broiler-houses and, when they're worked-out, put down. Such a party as I have in mind may very well trigger off a romance between – for instance – Miss F and Mr P. They are both of an age of discretion and, afterwards, they could take turn and

149

turn about at night, him reciting and her fantasizing. I don't like to think of Miss Foxberrow going to her grave not savouring the pleasures of love. Then, when the Major and I leave here, they could set up house in Sheltered Accommodation."

"If you are to be believed," I said, "although she may not have enjoyed the pleasures, at least she has endured the torments of love. Living with a murderer, I mean. After that, she may even find life with Mr Peplow dull for he is a gentlemanly person and, even if he had the inclination, long past attacking anyone."

The conversation then died of ennui.

Polly falls in Love

But this, by no means, was the end of approaching dissolution at no. 27.

"Who are these painter-chaps Ted took me to see yesterday?" Polly demanded. "And by the way, for the last time, let's forget Mariana; it slipped out yesterday, even though you promised. (Ted wants me to be called Natasha.) We were school-kids then. Waterland High was a bit of a dreamland, wasn't it?"

"But it was quite cheering at the time, wasn't it?" I suggested. "From what I have experienced during the past six weeks, the real world is not a patch on it. Ah, so you have been viewing the pre-Raphaelites. Are they not absolutely stunning?"

"No," she replied. "Why do their chaps look so constipated? And those droopy women with chests as flat as ironing-boards. Take that *Last of England* – they all look as though not a single one of them wanted to leave, so why didn't they stick it out here?"

"But Ted likes them."

"He may have done once," she said dismissively.

"Well then . . ." I began.

"But doesn't any more," she added smugly. "He prefers the Real Thing, which is me; he says I'm his magic sugar-lump."

"Ah!" I commented enigmatically. "That is his ultimate declaration of love. Rest easy, dear: he is in your power."

"He licks me, she confided. "And says if only I'll go for a weekend in Kidderminster, he'll want to lick me all over."

"Ah, beware!" I cautioned. "Licking now, biting later!"

"That Miss Foxberrow in Room One . . ." she said. "Is it really true what Mrs Gilpin-Jones says – that her guy was hung? How awful!"

"Quite untrue!"

"Then why didn't you contradict her yesterday? You were there when she told me."

"One's education is never complete" I replied.

"And what does that mean?" she complained.

"What is that bauble you are supporting around your waist?" I asked, spying the slave-chain once proferred me.

"Ted says it's something special he wants me in but I do wish it didn't jangle. He says it does something for him but won't say what."

"I can guess" I said grimly.

She turned to the wardrobe mirror and rehearsed languorous undulations, interspersed with eye-flashes.

"Is it wrong, Hetty, do you suppose" (she asked rhetorically), "Is it terribly wrong to dote upon oneself?"

I meet Mother again

Although it was only a 50 pence corporation bus-ride to Sutton Coldfield, as I stepped off and looked around, I knew that I was a long long way from Osokosie and Jordans Bank or, for that matter, from No. 27 and the Inner City.

The folk strolled placidly about. 'This is a very desirable location,' was writ large upon their faces. 'There are no blacks to speak of and only the odd Paki trying to get planning-permission for a grocer's shop which our Council will find legal reasons for refusing. And the Chief Constables of our buffer counties have forced the hippy convoys back into Wales where the natives, being much of a kind, can the better put up with them. And the unemployed and their minders are penned in West Brom and the Black Country. Life would be utter bliss but for the kids next door screaming in their swimming pool.'

They recognized that I was not one of them: Rose's ministrations on my person had failed yet again. 'We like it here,' they stared coldly, 'But there are quite enough of us here already. I suppose you needed to come up for air: well, now that you have had some, disappear to wherever you burrowed up from.'

At the estate agent's corner (*ALL OUR PROPERTIES HAVE SUN MAXIMIZATION*), I turned into Park Drive and then into the Park.

She was looking mutinous.

"You're late," she said crossly.

"But not too late. You are here still."

"What do you want this time? And I hope it's the last."

"My!" I said ironically. "You are a one for getting down to

business. Cannot we have a little mother-and-grown-up-daughter chat? I shall begin. You must like living here in Sutton Coldfield, Mummy?"

"We have nice neighbours."

"Ah, do you? But will you not concede that lots of them look as though they may be here just for the dying facilities? I am only making conversation."

"You do come out with the oddest things," she said. "You didn't get it from me. He always looked on the unpleasant side of things too. I suppose it comes from too much education."

"That is an interesting speculation," I agreed. "My father I presume?"

She did not answer but blushed.

"And where are my sister and little brother this afternoon?" I asked. "What a happy fellow he is to be sure. So high-spirited! This massive bruise is where the little brute kicked me."

"They are invited to a birthday party. I shall call for them," she replied, looking almost happy, before continuing spitefully, "They have their own little playmates and treats — picnics, conjurors, that sort of thing. When they are a little older we shall buy them a pony, and, in the long holidays, I expect they'll mess about in boats."

"Ah, like *Swallows and Amazons*," I suggested.

"Who?" she said, leaking self-confidence again. "Swallows and who?"

"Oh never mind," I said. "Just some other useless thing which comes from too much education. But I had to fill in the time somehow at Jordans Bank during the dearth of picnics, conjurors and ponies. Both the front and back gardens at Osokosie were given over to feeding us. One can hardly arrange a party on a cinder path . . . Osokosie was my late home (I added). And, anyway one of Mr Birtwisle's many tenets was that parties not only cost money but that happiness is noisy. By the way, have you told your new husband about me?"

"He is not my *new* husband," she replied indignantly. "He is my only husband: your father and I did not marry." And, rousing herself, she bounced back from the ropes and put in a shrewd blow which sent me reeling.

"You are an illegitimate," she snapped.

It took me a moment or two to get my wind back.

"You did not answer my question. Have you told him?"

"Certainly not."

(We were sparring briskly again.)

Cleverly she foresaw my next move, "At the right time I might tell," she said, "and of course he will accept it."

"After throwing a tantrum?"

"Well, yes," she admitted reluctantly. "I suppose so."

"What about his parents?"

"Not them," she replied bitterly. "With them Miles has to be first in everything."

"I suppose I can leave them out of it," I said magnanimously. "Him too – unless I have to."

She could not bring herself to thank me for this concession: in fact, she glowered and I felt that now was the moment to deliver the coup-de-grace.

"How much?" I asked casually.

"What?"

"How much is it worth for me to go away. And, this time, not come back?"

"Oh you little beast," she cried. "That's blackmail. I shall go to the police."

"Rubbish!" I said calmly. "I am your daughter – Sarah the First – asking for an allowance to see me through college. Blackmail indeed! Think of all the money I have saved you on ponies and parties."

She could not answer the unanswerable and bit her lips. She was staggering yet wouldn't throw in the sponge.

"Then I must call on them first. His folks," I said and rose to leave.

She couldn't take any more and began to blub.

"Marriage can be difficult," she sobbed. "I should know. I hope it happens to you some day so that you'll understand."

She was in a cruel predicament and, had I been able to detach myself from the past, might have felt sorry for her. But there was a tiny bundle being pushed over the adoption society's counter and a Mr and Mrs Birtwisle waiting to grab it.

"You don't know how spiteful his mother can be: he tells her everything," she bleated. "And what about Sarah and little Adam if they should find out?"

"What do I care for the little snobs," I said. "It would do that monster a world of good to believe that you might give him away too."

"I could manage five pounds each month," she said hopefully. "Well, maybe ten pounds."

"No fear. You cannot buy me off by instalments. I shall have a thousand pounds. Cash too. No cheques that can be stopped. One thousand."

"A thousand!"

"You can raid the kiddies' piggy-bank. And then, if you are still short – try robbing a real bank. Same time, same place, a week today. And don't forget – Cash down."

And I left.

But as I boarded the bus I remembered the shawl with a silver brooch and its aquamarine.

And I began to blub too.

The Major's Wedding

The wedding went off rather well. Matthew had become so popular since his near suicidal intervention in the riot that, despite the hour, St Barnabas's fielded a scratch choir and we could have had the bells too but for fear of summoning the beer-bellies who might have thrown things as we came out.

Polly looked dewy-eyed and managed a sob or two. "Oh Mummy would have been so happy," she faltered. "As she lay dying her one thought was for Grandpa's happiness. Her last words were, 'Be a good man, Daddy. Be a religious man'."

"But Polly," I muttered. "Did not Sir Walter Scott say that as *he* was dying? To his son-in-law, Lockhart?"

"Really! Did he? Shhh – we should be praying: Matthew is looking cross."

But, no sooner were we singing, than she began again.

"Be quiet, Polly," I hissed. "This is one of my favourite hymns."

> *'Through all the Changing Scenes of Life*
> *In trouble or in joy. . . .'*

I sang fervently, with a thought running through my head, This could have been written with me in mind. I certainly am experiencing several changes of scene and mostly troubled ones. Nevertheless when we reached,

> *'When in distress to him I called*
> *He to my rescue came,'*

doubts assailed me. There was the wrestling match with Mr

Birtwisle, there was Ronnie's betrayal, there was my ordeal at the hands of roller-skaters . . . need I say more?

The reception surpassed the ceremony. Rose had taken an upper room at the Steam Locomotive and had brought in caterers for the wedding breakfast. Speeches were made, toasts drunk, there was much uneasy gaiety. And Miss Foxberrow fell asleep and even lavish offers of food and drink could not arouse her. To us residents this was not extraordinary, because, of course, during the night watches she had been wide awake. But it brought on what follows.

"Poor old thing," Rose said sententiously. "It's all been a trifle overpowering for her. I do hope she's having pleasant dreams and not nightmares of that terrible scoundrel George Harpole who beat her and was hung."

"Harpole?" exclaimed the Major whose hearing-aid had disconcertingly widened his world. "Did you say George Harpole, dearest? I knew a George Harpole in the Yeomanry. Got an MC at Salerno. First rate officer! Knew his duty! And performed it, b'Gad! Hung him? Did you say they'd hung him? Harpole hung? They'd never hang Harpole. Can't be the same chap. My Harpole would never have got himself hung. Chap was soul of kindness. Bold as a lion in action, mild as a lamb in the Mess. Absolutely splendid fellow! Why would anyone want to hang George Harpole?"

His distress was manifest.

"They must have hung him pretty smartly: why only last Christmas we had a card from him. Polly dear, last Christmas, we did have a card from Captain Harpole? Yes, she says, we did. Thought we did. Robin perched on a holly sprig, wasn't it, Polly? Yes, she says, it was. Had the idea they weren't going to hang any more Englishmen. Only the Irish. Mind you, looking round this district, Rose. it's my belief Government's jumped the gun. Well none of us can help where we live."

I directed a long look at Rose. She, already weakened by the coals of fire heaped upon her by Matthew having arranged such a nice service for his supplanter, was in a tizzy (which rather became her).

"Well, it's only what I was told," she protested. "I don't think for a single minute there's a scrap of truth in it. Yes, indeed, I've always known it to be malicious rubbish and have said so many a time, haven't I, Hetty dear? In fact, I'm sure it was another Harpole or maybe Harper or Harpley. Yes that was him – Harper – and it was with a bread-knife. Certainly not Miss Foxberrow's Captain Harpole MC, dear."

"Of course, you are right (as you always are)," the Major said. "I recall now that they did hang a Harper. But it was a hacksaw he used not a breadknife, sweetheart. What a sensible little body you are."

At this Rose simpered, as well she might at being described not only as 'sensible and always likely to be right' but also as 'little'. But surely, I thought, she understands that he is using that Edwardian diminutive 'little' meaning 'a harmless homebody who knows her place in a man's world'?

"Ought to know Harpole if anyone does, since we were lads together in Lincolnshire. Went off to be an usher in some school somewhere. Saw nothing of him till the War. Matter of fact, seen nothing of him since. Got an invitation to his wedding but couldn't go. Then to the bride's funeral: couldn't attend that either. Then to another wedding. Chap seems to be everlastingly getting married. Tell you what I'll do, dearest, I'll write him a stiff letter and, if the fellow's free again, tell him to come at the double and do what's right by your Miss Foxberrow. Always knew his duty did Harpole. Wager a guinea the chap hasn't twigged she's still in the land of the living. Probably been trying to get in touch for years. Will have had adverts in *The Telegraph*. Probably cost him a small fortune. Anyway I want him to meet you Rosie, sweetheart. And if he doesn't fancy Miss Foxberrow, wouldn't mind if he asked me for the hand of little Polly here."

I glanced at Polly and grinned.

> *'I would not love thee half so much*
> *Lov'd I not Miss Foxberrow more.'*

I murmured. She did not find this amusing, turned away and began to display before Ted who had poked his nose in uninvited.

A Visit from Miss Braceburn

As I was learning is common in life, one disturbance to orderly arrangements followed fast on the heels of another for, on the following Friday, Miss Braceburn, recuperating from her horrifyingly bracing holiday with the gym mistress, turned up.

"Oh I bear glad tidings, Hetty," she announced. "Glorious news indeed − I have arranged an interview at my old Cambridge college which of course is the *only* place for you. You must remember my telling you of the Prolocutor of the English Literature Schools − Professor Massinger (who, of course, I knew as 'Hugh') − oh, Hetty, he was great."

"Why, Miss Braceburn?" I asked.

"Why?" she repeated, puzzled.

"Yes, why is Professor Massinger great?"

"Yes, of course, you are right. 'Great!' Dear me! At Waterland High one so easily picks up such generalizations."

(Like 'magic', I murmured.)

"Hugh breathed fire into his teaching," she exclaimed loudly. "Even into John Milton."

"I should have thought Milton had fire enough without the

necessity of being stirred up by Mr Massinger's bellows," I said drily. "And several hundred Miltonic lines of raging flame might be all too consuming for most of us."

Miss Braceburn considered this and modified her ecstasies.

"And his voice," she went on. "Such undertones of sensibility; when he spoke of Shelley, one knew that one was seeing Shelley plain."

She looked quite rapt now, far, far from Waterland High and Brumbrum.

> *"She is far from the land*
> *Where her dead hero lies."*

I quoted – but not aloud.

"He must have influenced you much, Miss Braceburn," I said.

"I would have done anything, yes anything for him," she breathed (now only marginally with me). "Anything at all!"

From this I supposed that she meant doing anything the Governors of Waterland High certainly would have sacked her for doing.

I leafed across my male acquaintances to date – Sonny, Ronnie, Ted, Ivan, Matthew . . . none aroused any such feeling of self-sacrifice. No, not even Douglas. "After Cambridge, Waterland High must seem a let-down," I suggested.

"I shall not be there for ever," she declared, "I have almost completed my primum opus. When it is published, any university worth its salt will welcome me with a fellowship. Have I not mentioned it before? No? It is provisionally entitled *Beauty is not Enough* and advances a proposition that any work of literature lacking the moral force which informs and ennobles Robert Browning should be expunged from school curricula. It is something about which I feel deeply."

We considered this: Miss Braceburn perhaps uneasily wondering if such expense of spirit might not have been a thief of time.

"Now," she said briskly. "Tell me what you have been doing?"

And I held nothing back and told her about the meetings with my mother.

"Oh!" she said when I had been heard out. "Things have not been easy for you, Hetty, and many another would not have kept faith with her own inalienable self as you have done. This does you much credit."

"Yes, but what should I do?" I asked rather desperately.

"Ah," she replied. "That is not easily answered. Now what would Robert Browning have advised, I wonder. . . . Let us look again at his *Abt Vogler,*

> *All we have willed or hop'd or dreamed of good shall exist –*
> *Not its semblance but itself.*

"There," she said earnestly, "There is your answer."

But later that evening, I thought, Oh yes that is all very well: you have not been through the mill like me. No one handed you across a counter like a parcel of groceries. You have lived life at second-hand. And Bob Browning – what did he know about things as they really are, life as it really is!

And I went comfortless and late to my bed, so that Mr Peplow was well advanced into his repertory and chanting across night and silence,

> *By the shores of Gitche Goome,*
> *By the Shining Big Sea Water,*
> *Stood the wigwam of Nokomis,*
> *Daughter of the Moon, Nokomis.*
> *Dark behind it rose the forest,*
> *Rose the dark and gloomy pine trees*

161

I suppose what I am going through, I reflected gloomily, is the dark night of the soul.

I then fell asleep.

I lose a Mother

She was waiting miserably for me, loitering uneasily by the now familiar bench in the park and looking peekish.

"I've brought it," she said, fumbling in her handbag. There's £750 here in ten pound notes and I swear that I'll send you the rest poste restante to wherever you say. Please believe me. But you must give me another week or two so that I can borrow the money in dribs and drabs. Then, you see, I shan't have to explain why I need it. And you will keep your promise, won't you? About not coming back. You've not changed your mind? Honestly I can't stand much more. He's beginning to suspect that I'm upset about something. And you did promise."

"Oh please don't worry your little head," I exclaimed, irritated by this double reminder that I was someone she wished never to see again. "I'm not one who breaks her word. You can rely upon me," and added bitterly, "And so can any baby who comes my way; she or he can rely upon me too."

And the while I was thinking, This is a mother begging her daughter to go away and never return. It is truly staggering. When, later, I tell Rose, she will not believe me. And this idea was so awful that I began to tremble. Then I nudged myself, Oh come on Hetty, no weepies. Please! This human-being, this woman, really *does* believe that she owes you . . . not even a flutter of her eyelashes. Not even that. Well, my girl, take the cash and Amen, so be it.

And I pocketed the bundle of notes.

"Aren't you going to count it?" she asked fearfully.

"I shrugged. "If it's not all there, you will hear from me. Oh dear! You are a pathetic creature, aren't you? I suppose that your husband has found you out and gives you a bad time now and then. No, no, I do not mean that he's found out about *me*. About *you*."

I had hit a sore spot and her face twitched.

And now that it was all over she was torn between hopping it and a blood-is-thicker-than-water curiosity about the baby who had come back, the grown-up daughter (albeit an extortioner) she would never set eyes on again.

"What will you do now?" And forced out a 'dear'.

"You have no cause to worry," I replied airily. "You can't possibly suppose that I shall return to the people you foisted me upon. I know where I am going and have true friends to help me there."

"But you're only eighteen," she sniffed.

"Ah, so you've not forgotten when you had me then? Well done! Then you will be happy to learn that I have excellent A-levels and expect to be offered a place at Cambridge. (I suppose that I shall not be running into my father there?) Yes," I went on, rubbing it in, "I am the flower of the flock. And you know it. Yet you kept those two little snobs and gave me away."

"But how will you manage? At Cambridge? Clothes and train-fares and books. . . ."

"I have managed so far," I said. "I had to manage. Oh what a flab you are! You must have a swinging brick where the rest of us hang our hearts. If you had had a spark of love in you, you would have walked out on your beastly folks. And with me in your arms. Others have done it and found men who were proud of them for hanging on to their babies. There was a programme on Channel 4 only last week. . . ."

"I saw it too," she muttered. "It made me cry and he wanted to know why. I thought, If only I had my chance again."

Hearing this made me so furious that I could have shaken her. "What!" I just about shouted. "Your chance? You have had your *second* chance. When I turned up three weeks ago you could have taken me along and said to him, "Look here, Edward, or Peter, or Miles, or whatever his name is. Look, this is my girl. This is the real Sarah. And she is coming to live with us. Kick up a fuss and we shall leave and the pair of us will manage as best we may. But manage we shall.

"But you were a miserable coward. And you still are one."

By this time she was in an awful state. "I could kill myself," she whined.

"Pooh!" I said (sounding uncomfortably like Miss Braceburn). "Pooh! Now stop snivelling and tell me about my father."

"Oh no! I can't do that."

"And why not, pray?"

"It wouldn't be fair."

"Fair! Fair to who? To *whom?*"

"Him."

"Why him? What about me? Am I the only ball to be punted around in this game? He had his fun and here I am. So, should I need further economic support until I find my feet, it would be as well to know where to apply.

"Oh, how entertaining it will be to come upon him (let's say) on the Wedding Day of yet another fruit of his loins! 'Hello Daddy!' I shall say. 'What, you don't remember me? Really! But, of course, you never saw me, did you? You sloped off and left poor little Wendy back in Sutton Coldfield holding the baby (and I don't mean that metaphorically). Your precious career . . . of course that couldn't be prejudiced, could it? You still do not know me? I am the

164

bride's elder sister – the child who was put on offer. But here I am – bright, well-spoken, not unduly weather-beaten after being so long adrift – in fact, don't you agree, quite presentable. So would you not like to present me to my siblings? Wouldn't that be fun, Daddy?' "

"Oh really!" my mother exclaimed, half-scandalized, half tickled at the idea (growing in attraction) of him being shovelled his share of horror at my resurrection. And she even began to giggle.

"Now, tell me," I went on. "And let it be the truth. Who was he and where is he?"

"An undergrad," she replied. "Oxford – he was staying during their long vacation with Simon Winship. We met at the tennis club. I knew him for just that one month." And began to whimper.

"Oh, come on," I said sharply. "No self-pity, please, Stiff upper lip, Wendy. Remember that you are a daughter of the regiment."

"I don't know any more than that. He knew about you but wouldn't do the decent thing. Daddy threatened him but he said he'd go to court and swear it wasn't his."

"It?" I snarled.

"You, then. And they couldn't face it being reported in the papers. So I was sent away to have you. To Droitwich Spa. It was terrible."

And she hung her head.

Poor frightened creature, I thought, packed off to kennels and only let back when the coast was clear. Whilst he skulked somewhere, waiting for a court-order which never came. The stinker!

"Don't bother to tell me you haven't kept some sort of tabs on him. Where is he?"

"He's a professor of something or other I'm not sure where: he was very brainy."

She told me this half-bitterly, half proudly. Then she looked closely at me as though momentarily seeing someone else.

Ah, I thought, So you still remember him! And who knows – despite everything. . . . Oh how awful to be a woman!

"Thank you," I said. "There is nothing more that I wish to know. And now (standing up) the curtain is about to fall on our three act melodrama. This time you will be rid of me for good and all, for ever and ever, amen. Come, come, surely you can look more relieved than that? Oh, one last thing – What is your baking like? Particularly your caraway-seed cakes?"

"Whatever are you talking about," she exclaimed (nettled). "More intellectual impertinence, I suppose!"

I clutched the money. £750 not only felt comfortingly substantial – it sadly brought Miss Braceburn to mind. ('Oh Hetty dear, you cannot go through with this. . . . You would not be true to yourself. Think of R.B., dear.

> *So through the thunder comes a human voice,*
> *Saying "O heart I made, a heart beats here. . . .'*

Hetty, you simply cannot do it. Well, let us omit "simply": it is superfluous. Hetty, it wouldn't be *you,* dear.')

"Here is your money," I said fiercely and dropped the bundle into her lap. To keep it wouldn't be *me.* And it would remind me of *you."*

Then I turned and made for the park's exit.

But still I could hear her sobbing quietly and turned again. There was something about her bowed shoulders and bent head that tugged at the heart.

Oh please God, I begged, Spare me.

But he didn't, any more than he had not spared me from Mr Birtwisle's blows and Mrs Birtwisle's kisses, from the roller-skaters, from Miss Braceburn and from Robert Browning. So, weak at the knees (as seemed to be common in these moments of spiritual distress), I went back and put my arms around her.

"Look, Mum," I faltered, "I know that it wasn't like that at all. I knew it weeks ago when I was given the aquamarine that you left in my shawl. You did your best. Yes, you did, you did. And you gave me life. Thank you for that. And the little brooch; it's so lovely. I shall wear it on my Wedding Day.

Now come on. See me to the bus."

Then we kissed and cried a little.

Yet Another Parting

"All that has happened will take another form and substance as time passes," Miss Braceburn said gently as we sat in a surviving Kardomah Café munching caraway-seed cake and relishing the coffee every other establishment in Brum had forgotten how to make.

"Recall Willliam Wordsworth's obiter dicta. 'Poetry is the overflow of powerful feelings – emotion recollected in tranquillity.' As time moves forward and memory longingly looks back, it will be like that for you, Hetty."

"I suppose so, Miss Braceburn," I said, by no manner of means convinced.

"Hetty, it will, it will," she murmured with utter certitude. "And I am glad and proud that you behaved so very well. (As, of course, I knew you would.) You were true to yourself. Good girl!"

Then, properly alarmed to be seen tottering on the shaky fence between sentiment and mush, she hastily withdrew and called my attention to the cafe's gilding-metal repousée adornment. "Art Deco!" she told me approvingly. "About 1908, I should imagine. A local carryover from the Arts and Crafts Guild Movement of the early years of this century. There always are minor features of interest (casting an eye on Brumbrum's prevailing concrete) to leaven the most unpromising dough. And, of course, we must not forget those disregarded skilled craftsmen of this sometime home of James Watt, Edward Burne-Jones, Joseph Priestly and Thos. Baskerville . . . you found refuge in no mean city, Hetty.

"Do not harbour a grudge against life," she went on, lightly touching my hand as it bore a last morsel of cake mouthwards. A faint smile flitted across her dark face – "Recall our R.B. (and this for the last time),

> *Hatred and cark and care – what place have they*
> *In yon blue liberality of heaven?*

"Hetty, you have done well. In this circumstance I shall fall back on the vulgar colloquial usages of your regrettable friend, Polly Horbling – When the chips were down you showed us that you had spunk."

Once again she smiled momentarily. "Did I say 'for the last time'? No matter, I cannot resist the man. As (with minor help from the great W.S.) he puts it so well and, in your situation, most aptly,

> *Dauntless the slug-horn to my lips I pressed*
> *And blew, 'Childe Roland to the Dark Tower came.'*

"Thank you, Miss Braceburn," I said. "As a matter of fact, I had rather seen myself in that role."

"Now a little of myself before we part," she said. "I am changing my vocation. I shall not be returning to Waterland High. There is a Community of Poor Sisters under the Malverns who tolerate dawgs and where I shall become a religious (the word may be used both adjectivally and nominally, Hetty). And now, if I hasten, I shall catch the 11.27 – Mustafa is tied to a post on Platform 16. One utterly last thing, dear – your Cambridge interview – avoid mention of R.B. No, no, there is no time to explain. But work up an enthusiasm for Josef Conrad: Professor Massinger, Hugh, dotes on that boringly repetitive Pole. It is his one frailty."

I walked home. First Bennett's Hill, then across the Cathedral churchyard and, suppressing an upsurge of wrath at the brutish disregard of his last testament, 'Do not dig my bones into so-called sanctified earth,' gave poor Baskerville's headstone a propiatory pat. And up Soho Hill, along Victoria Street and the city's Gold, Silver and Jewellery Quatier, past the Sauce Works, poor Mr Williams's deserted Bookshop and across the still scarred Battlefield of St Barnabas's. Miss Braceburn had gone and my last of girlhood had gone with her – alas yet another 'changing scene of life'. . . . Ave atque vale.

A Hanged Man

I scarcely was in and ribbing runner-beans when someone knocked softly on the front door.

"Oh, don't let's answer it," Rose said huffily. "It's happened twice whilst you were out – one was Cavity Wall-fillings and the other Double-Glazing. 'You will be warm this winter, Madam,' he pleaded. 'Young man,' I told him, 'Nothing you can do could make this mausoleum warm. Here, we just pull on another cardigan and skirt at each temperature drop of ten degrees.' "

The knocking began again.

"Home-improvers on spec never knock twice," she said. "You had better see who it is, Hetty. Do not agree in writing to buy anything."

An old gentleman, very respectably turned out, was waiting on the doorstep and deferentially raised an antique but well-brushed bowler hat. "I do hope that I am not being a nuisance," he said. "This is no. 27? Yes? It is? Oh good! Thank you." And dried up: we gazed helplessly at one another.

"It is quite a pleasant day," I remarked. "Not so stuffy as many lately. I believe that the rain will keep off."

He shuffled his unusually large boots.

"Oh yes, you are quite right," he said with more decision.

"Yes I believe that it will. The rain! The countryside is looking very well – quite quite splendid in fact. Autumn was always my favoured season. As my train came along the Vale, the reds and yellows of the chestnuts and beeches about Alderton were glorious, yes quite glorious. I rarely have seen them in better form. Never in fact."

"Oh good!" I said.

And again we dried up whilst he fumbled at his ragged moustache. Oh come on man, I thought irritably. Out with it for goodness sake. I cannot linger here for ever: there is lunch to be got ready.

"As a matter of fact," he began and stopped.

"Yes?" I said helpfully.

"As a matter of fact, I am seeking a Miss Foxberrow" (intently examining my pinafore). "Yes . . . Miss Foxberrow. Miss Emma Foxberrow. You see – my name is Harpole. I am George Harpole. But I am afraid that Miss Foxberrow is not expecting me. You see I . . . well, the long and short of it is – this morning I received a letter from an old comrade-in-arms, Major Horbling."

"Oh good!" I cried warmly. "So he wrote to you, after all."

"You see I have come to take Miss Foxberrow away."

"Do come in, Mr Harpole," I cried, thinking how Rose was going to relish this encounter and already wondering how it could be arranged for me to witness a longed-for reunion of lost souls, "As a matter of fact I am not unfamiliar with the situation," I went on. "For Miss Foxberrow often speaks of you."

"Really!" he exclaimed. "Really! I am most gratified. This is splendid. Oh jolly good!"

"Chiefly at night."

"So she has explained things. This is much much better than I had hope of."

"Well, not exactly," I said (for already I had worked up a

warmth of feeling for him and knew that he must be told only the truth). "Miss Foxberrow talks about you to herself, you see. But, being slightly hard of hearing, she does not understand that she can be heard (involuntarily) in our entrance hall. One does not listen; but one cannot help hearing – if you follow me. I am so pleased that you have come, Mr Harpole, and know that you both will be so happy talking over old days in Tampling St Nicholas and by the lagoon at Sinji. By the way, who was that Mr Shutlanger who rose to glory on the day of your trial? And what offence had you committed? Well, perhaps not now but, before you go, if you would be kind enough to satisfy my friendly curiosity. . . .? And may I introduce myself – I am Miss Hetty Beauchamp, Mrs Gilpin-Jones's companion-help."

"Thank you, Miss Beauchamp," he said, earnestly shaking my hand but once more shuffling his large feet. "You are only a girl (and a very charming one, if I may say so) but you have caught hold of the right end of the stick. To tell you the truth, I fell deeply in love with Miss Foxberrow when I first set eyes on her. And, although I married twice, that is the condition in which I have remained. Not that Phyllis and I and, later, Penelope and I, were unhappy. We were devoted each to the other. Well – someday – you will understand, my dear. The heart, you know. . . ."

"A person of sensibility can understand such things very well, Mr Harpole," I reminded him. "Surely one does not need to touch flame to know that it will scorch. Is not this one of the proper rewards of a study of our literature?"

He gave a proper consideration to the observation. "Yes," he agreed. "It had never before occurred to me and, of course, you are right. Thank you. It was an ill-considered remark. I recall my own matriculation year, 1929, alas long long ago; the set verse book was a selection of the Works of Robert Browning – Karshish, A Toccata at Galuppi's, Abt

172

Vogler, Beautiful Evelyn Hope is Dead – and so on, that sort of thing. And, at the time, I recall thinking, Ah so life is like this, is it? (You see I was no more than sixteen and quite naïve.)"

As I already have said, I had liked him even as he shuffled uneasily on our doorstep. Now I looked at him with admiration.

"Exactly!" I agreed. "We have much in common, Mr Harpole, besides a distaste for verbal elision. Please wait here for a moment."

His face lit up. "Good girl!" he exclaimed. "Down with the can'ts and won'ts and don'ts, isn'ts and wouldn'ts!" disarmingly adding 'I once was a schoolmaster. But not a successful one I am afraid.'

Then I dashed to the kitchen.

"You had better come immediately, Rose," I whispered. "It is George Harpole risen from the dead and on our threshold in his grave-clothes."

"Whatever are you talking about, you silly goose," she said crossly. "And whoever was it at the door?"

"It is Mr Harpole," I repeated. "No, I am not dreaming. It is, it is. He has come for Miss Foxberrow. Yes *that* Mr Harpole – the chap you used to say they hung."

She had the grace to flush.

"Then show him into Room One," she said decisively. "Give me a moment or two to titivate and I shall follow."

I preceded our visitor, announcing, "Miss Foxberrow, Mr George Harpole is here."

"Oh, thank you, Hetty," she replied calmly. "When I awoke I knew that this was the day. No, do not ask me how. As you can see, I am packed and ready."

And so she was. There were several leather suitcases and, draped across them, a valuable mink coat which I had not seen before, and a straw hat with a silk red rose stuck cockily in its ribbon.

Then she turned and said, "Well, George, neither of us has grown any younger. As you see, I am an old wreck."

A most touching scene then occurred. George Harpole strode forward and manfully took her in his arms and gave her the sort of kisses Ted had grumbled about, old fashioned ones, first on her brow and then upon her lips. "I have arranged for a taxi to call at two o'clock, Emma darling, so that we can catch the 2.30 train, with time enough and to spare," he said masterfully.

"Emma, you will like Quince Tree Cottage upon Bredon Hill. The Severn River may be seen from our kitchen window and, in the other direction, beyond Mr Archer's farm buildings, the Malverns, and over to the south, the Cotswold Hills. And from our bedroom window there is. . . ."

"Oh George!" she quavered, "You always were one for everlastingly listing details and eventualities and now you are going on like a Sunday newspaper travel guide. In a moment you will be telling me 'the bells they sound so clear'. For some time at least, it is only you I shall want to look at."

Meanwhile, she was smiling knowingly over his shoulder. And winked. No, there was no mistaking this for Rose saw it too. She winked. Then we left them together for (let the heavens fall) there was lunch to be got on with. But I was much encouraged by yet another reminder of how romantic and absolutely glorious life could be – even when we have one foot in the grave.

Mr Peplow — Farewell!

Things were moving with unnerving speed. For instance, Rose had changed her mind and told the Major about Reg.

"Oh Hetty," she said rapturously. "What did I tell you? He always was an extraordinary man and now with his hearing-aid, he is a new one. He immediately told me, 'Can understand how the poor fellow misses you and longs to be back, God rest his soul. But can't have him hanging around. We'll move off and leave him where he lived his happiest hours.'"

"Did he say where?" I asked. "Where he is going to remove you to?"

"We have been leased a cottage at a peppercorn rent by the Major's brother-in-law who is a gentleman-farmer in a little picture postcard spot called Steeple Sinderby. Oh you will like it, dear — for of course you must make your home with us. No, now let's have no nonsense. Polly insists. And you know the Major is very fond of you. As for me, after all we have been through together, you don't need to be told how I value your companionship. And I promise that I'll never tell a soul about the roller-skating."

"But can you settle in the country, Rose?" I asked doubtfully. "It is summer there for only short periods, you know. And people can be very nosey and censorious. And there are more draughts even than here. . . ." And left it at that.

"I shall find things to do," she asserted stoutly. "The Major tells me that Mrs Fangfoss (his sister, dear) is of a literary bent and he would like me to try my hand along similar lines. I shall write a novel: enough has happened to me to fill half-a-dozen of the damned things."

When later I confided this to Polly, she laughed coarsely.

"Wait till she finds what goes on at Towlers End. Did Grandpa mention Poor Beatie! And that ogre Fangfoss!. . . . And have you heard that Matthew's leaving St Barnabas? He told me solemnly that his Sierra Leone Propogation of the Gospel in Heathen Lands Society had written off Brumbrum and cut off funds. So he's taken a nice little parish in Sussex with some very nice regular elderly churchgoers. Can't fathom why he looks so hangdog. Just the place to pick up an open-minded, healthy colonel's daughter, I should have thought."

"Or do you mean 'a colonel's open-minded healthy daughter'?" I asked automatically. "Or perhaps 'an open-minded colonel's healthy daughter'?"

"Oh Hetty, there are times when you are so irritating," she snapped. "Let us hope that, in time, you will grow out of your education. Oh and I almost forgot to tell you . . . that woman in Room Seven whom we've scarcely seen, the one who for some odd reason or other, bicycled across Turkestan dressed as a boy . . . she left an hour ago, declaring that she was off to cross somewhere else."

I went off to scale the heights and take this news of unsettling activity to Mr Peplow. "I expect that I shall be sold with the house," he told me. "No, really Hetty, I do not mind in the least. And that is nothing at all to do with growing old: coming to think of it, I always must have had an inclination to take whatever comes as it came. And to put up with it.

"As far as I can recall I only once tried to give life a push the way I wanted it to go. Long, long ago. But, of course, when it came to a point, I couldn't bring myself to do what needed to be done. Yet, oddly enough, someone else did it for me. And good came of it. Yes, much good. I shall never forget Hilda's face when I returned. Yet when I caught the train that morning it seemed to be the end for me.

"Bear that in mind, Hetty girl. Never neglect to keep in

176

mind the worst mess you ever found yourself. Then you always can console yourself that, whatever your current plight, it cannot be worse than that. Weeping may endure for a night, my girl, but joy cometh in the morning."

Mr Peplow had a very reassuring smile, an 'all thy waves and billows have gone over me' smile and I resolved to cultivate something along the same lines.

And, later, as, for the last time, I drowsed off in my Brumbrum attic, he began to gravely recite through our party wall, 'Not a drum was heard. . . .' (Ah, how I would miss those noble lines!)

> *'Slowly and sadly we laid him down*
> *From the field of his fame fresh and gory.*
> *We carved not a line or raised not a stone*
> *But we left him alone in his glory.'*

And very proper, too, I thought. Well done, Edward Peplow! Well done! It suits the occasion admirably. And then (with my late employment in St Tobit's churchyard in mind) − Far better a shining and abiding glory than a monument in even best quality undertaker's marble.

The Secret Sharer

The further that I advanced from its railway station, Cambridge provided more and more to inform and to admire and less and less to relate to Jordans Bank or to Birmingham. For example, there seemed to be no prevailing species of native, for whereas true Fenlanders can be distinguished by their clenched teeth (to keep out the east wind) and their flickering eyes (to watch no one gets more than themselves) and almost all Brummies look stunned at the Progress wreaked upon their city, those folk thronging Cambridge thoroughfares were either Mid-Eastern Orientals or house-trained intellectuals from elsewhere who had given up the struggle to fulfil bright hopes promised by schoolmasters in their exam-ridden youth.

"No . . . yes . . . well, you are both wrong and right," an elderly perspicacious gentleman explained as we rubbed shoulders on a Trinity Street antiquarian bookseller's fourth floor. "Cambridge has its aborigines but, apart from a few mid-winter weeks, they keep to themselves in reservations away from the river and the quads. I am told that they hate the tourist hordes, ridiculously believing that they are wearing out their ancient town by staring at it."

He then kindly saw me on my way to Miss Braceburn's old college. "Good fortune attend you," he said as we parted. "Yes, good fortune indeed young woman! Many a long year ago, I too came here on a similar mission. But take warning from my fate: as you see, I am still here. Now, may I offer counsel? – eschew irrelevance, look your inquisitor squarely in the eye, hazard his opinions and discreetly echo them. Then, if an opportunity presents itself, feign familiarity with as many respectable books that are not on your syllabus as come to mind." He bowed graciously and told me that he had greatly enjoyed our brief encounter.

I was not kept waiting. A tall rangey man (but no longer so slim as described by Miss B) wearing a countryman's check viyella shirt and with a splendidly flaming head of hair, seated me before him and invited me to be at ease (I quote).

"Ah yes," he said wearily, patting the bright blue and red-spotted tie (which signalled his literary calling) and putting on half-moon spectacles, "Ah yes, of course, now let me see – Miss Anstey?"

"No," I replied, "She is another."

178

"Perhaps that is just as well," he said drily (to put me down) because I see that we have decided not to offer her a place."

He then gave me a swift Are-we-going-to-have-trouble-with-you look. And this I received wide-eyed and encouragingly.

"No," I said helpfully. "I am Miss H. L. Beauchamp. From Waterland."

He rummaged for a pipe and struck it several sharp blows against the edge of his desk: the friendly uncle act was slipping.

"Ah yes, indeed yes – here we are. Beaumont H. L."

"Miss Hetty Lucasta Beauchamp," I said.

"Lucasta?" he repeated desperately. "Lucasta?"

"Lucasta! *To Lucasta on going to the Wars.* 'I could not love thee, Dear, so much, loved I not honour more.' That Lucasta."

He pulled himself together.

"And you are from – ah, Waterland Comprehensive?"

"High," I corrected. "We have not yet surrendered."

" I see from this accompanying letter that your English teacher, Miss Braceburn . . . Braceburn? I had a student, Sidonie Braceburn . . . in the mid-seventies. Remind me of your Miss Braceburn please."

"At Waterland High, she was considered to have an interesting appearance," I replied. "She also moved at an unusually brisk pace."

"Yes, of course, of course. She took astonishingly long strides. Loped. Yes, she loped. She was a high-minded young woman. Sidonie took a very good degree. Well, that I suppose is neither here nor there. Miss Beaumont, which author of novels do you most favour?"

He asked this patronisingly and plainly would not have given a fig had I nominated Mickey Spillane.

"Oh, Josef Conrad! Since he was brought to our notice whilst in the Fourth Form, I have been much taken by him."

"Really!" he exclaimed suspiciously. "Usually he is more favoured· by growing lads fretting to circumnavigate the globe. You have a particular novel in mind?"

"Oh indeed, yes," I enthused. *Lord Jim!* I am impressed by its moral tone. It tells of a young merchant-naval officer who. . . ."

"Yes, yes, I know the story," he interrupted, tetchily making it clear who was the Conrad authority present.

"Yes," I went on. "Jim's lapse from honour to save his skin! It is a Tale of Betrayal. And of Redemption."

"Betrayal . . . and redemption," he echoed suspiciously.

"Yes," I added daringly, "It is a theme which appeals to me – honour besmirched and. . . ."

"Yes?" he said uneasily.

"And honour redeemed," I added firmly.

He sought narrowly for a sign of impertinence, but I had assumed the wide-eyed helpful look long ago highly developed to frustrate Mr Birtwisle (regretting that Polly was not present to admire it).

"Yes, yes," he said testily. "Quite so! Honour besmirched and (did you say?) Honour redeemed. Facile, perhaps a trifle facile! Simplistic, yes?"

He thought for a while, tapping a pencil on his teeth.

"Your interest in Conrad intrigues me," he said, adding sardonically, "You do not (by chance) identify with any of his characters? Captain Lingard's beautiful, half-wild daughter in *The Outcast of the Islands*, for instance? The thought crosses my mind."

"Oh no," I replied. "His women, with rare exception, are poor sorts of creature. They do little more than respond – empty echoes of their men."

"Ah," he said enigmatically and began to tap his teeth

again. "Perhaps one of his male characters then?"

(There was no doubt about it; it was him all right. The same dark skin, the same hair . . .)

"Oh yes," I said, pulling myself together, "And, what with one thing and another, particularly at this time, perhaps his *Secret Sharer.*"

"*Secret Sharer!*" he murmured. "Please remind me."

"Oh, the final few lines — 'a free spirit, a proud swimmer striking out for a new destiny'."

" 'Striking out for a new destiny,' eh?" he repeated, bemused. "Mmmmm . . . so perhaps, young woman, you feel that your fate, your destiny, your fulfilment, may be here in this university?"

"That is not for me to say," I answered modestly whilst, at the same time, thinking, Great heavens, he is beginning to sound like Conrad himself — 'your fate, your destiny, your fulfilment'!

"Well, Miss . . . ah, Beauchamp, your excellent A-levels confirmed (this grimly) by your informed enthusiasm for the more moral works of Josef Conrad, justify a belief that this College may offer you a place."

He paused and gazed at me with a wild surmise but with a deal less confidence than did stout Cortez ('silent upon his peak in Darien').

"Yes, certainly! In principle, that is. Categorically! (He was in full retreat.) Look here — we *are* offering you a place."

"Thank you, Professor," I said. "And I am happy to accept it."

"Now, let me see. Your guardian? Ah, Rose Gilpin-Jones! Not Beauchamp? No father? The War? No, no, he would have been too young. . . ."

"He had gone before. Before I knew him, that is," I admitted looking as suitably downcast as had Polly when describing her mother's deathbed.

"I am very sorry," he said but not looking so. "Well, I am sure he would have been pleased to know that you are coming to us."

He stood up, the better to be rid of me. And I knew in my bones that he was nagging his subconscious to shoot me to its surface. He was thinking. Why is this girl's face so disturbingly familiar? Wherever have I seen it before?

And I thought back, You saw it whilst shaving this morning.

"Then that is all," he said. "Thank you . . . Miss Beauchamp. We shall meet again in October."

I turned towards the door.

"Simplistic, perhaps, don't you think?" he murmured.

I turned again. "Professor?" I said.

" 'Honour besmirched . . . and honour redeemed' " he said. Simplistic, eh? Well, never mind. . . .A very good day to you."

I closed his door. And, as I left the building, announced quite loudly to sparrows scattering before me on the lawns, "Yes, a very good day indeed. An unusually good day! I can see that I shall savour Cambridge. And Cambridge me. Ah – but what of you, Professor?"

Then, hurrying railway-wards in the bright sunshine and marvelling at the lively times which lay before me, I paused and scrutinized myself reflectively in a shop window. For I had learned that life was not like literature and it had taken me a deal less time than Don Quixote to discover this. Life could not be relied upon. Life was unpredictable. Life swung wildly and without meaning from this to that. And little happened as one had a right to expect it to happen.

And, as I walked on beneath the chestnut trees now turning towards autumn, I had a not unpleasing feeling that my struggles were by no means over but about to begin again.

Polly was waiting impatiently by the station entrance and

both of us must have been reminded of that long gone morning when I shook Fenland's mud from off my shoes because, without a word, we began to giggle and then to laugh loudly. So, arm in arm, we strolled off down the long platform in the warm sunshine carolling gaily,

'Tous les jeunes filles et garçons amoureuses,
Tous les garçons et les filles de mon age . . .

Sherburn-in-Elmet
and
Anners
and Milldale Road.
September 1st 1987